Windswept

Windswept

A Novel

Kate Hancock

Kate Hancock

SUNSTONE
PRESS

SANTA FE

Sunstone books may be purchased for educational, business, or sales promotional use.
For information please write: Special Markets Department, Sunstone Press,
P.O. Box 2321, Santa Fe, New Mexico 87504-2321.

Cover art › Fred J. Hancock
Book and Cover design › Vicki Ahl
Body typeface › Adobe Jenson Pro
Printed on acid-free paper
∞
eBook 978-1-61139-290-6

Library of Congress Cataloging-in-Publication Data

Hancock, Kate, 1950-
   Windswept : a novel / by Kate Hancock.
     pages cm
   ISBN 978-0-86534-998-8 (softcover : alk. paper)
   1. Widows--Fiction. 2. Families--Fiction. 3. Victims of terrorism--Fiction.
   4. Domestic fiction. I. Title.
   PS3608.A69825W56 2014
   813'.6--dc23
                                   2014016480

WWW.SUNSTONEPRESS.COM
SUNSTONE PRESS / POST OFFICE BOX 2321 / SANTA FE, NM 87504-2321 /USA
(505) 988-4418 / ORDERS ONLY (800) 243-5644 / FAX (505) 988-1025

Dedication

For every child who has lost a parent through senseless violence and for the mothers and fathers who have put aside their own grief and given their children the strength and courage to heal.

Prologue

Chappaquiddick, Martha's Vineyard Island, Massachusetts
October, 1796

Josiah Cooke was not a man who worried a great deal. After all, a worrier would never have brought a young wife all the way from England to the far end of an island where the nearest neighbors were miles away across a swiftly moving channel. No, Josiah Cooke was not a worrier—but he *was* worried tonight.

Josiah Cooke was a farmer who grew crops to feed his wife and himself and enough to take to market when times were good. He had four good milkers and a sturdy bull, Samson. Now, dairy cows are creatures of habit. After the morning milking, they go out to the field and when it's time to be milked in the evening, they come back to the barn. Tonight, Josiah went out to bring his "girls" into the barn and was dismayed to see that there were only three. Ruth, Esther and Debra had returned as expected, but Delilah, who if the truth be told was always a bit ornery, had not returned with the others.

Normally, this would not have been terribly worrisome to Josiah, but Delilah was coming near the time to give birth to the calf she was carrying. Cows about to give birth often wandered off to be alone, but if there was a problem with the birth, no one would be there to help. Josiah needed the calf to be born healthy in order to expand his herd, so it fell to him to go out and find the wayward Delilah. It was just bad luck that a thunderstorm was moving toward the island from the northeast.

With a coil of rope over his shoulder and carrying a lantern, Josiah kissed his wife and set out to find his missing cow. Not far from his small cabin, Josiah felt the first spatters of rain. Looking out across the sound, Josiah saw huge roiling black clouds racing towards him. He quickened his pace, calling as he went, "Delilah—hooo, hooo, hooo—Delilah!"

He had gone perhaps half a mile into the coarse dune grass when the storm struck in earnest. The wind-driven rain came in torrents. Thunder crashed about him and lightning lit up the sky. Josiah continued to call Delilah, but the noise from the storm made it all but impossible to hear anything. As he pushed his way through the waist high grass, Josiah thought how mournful the wind sounded as it moaned and shrieked and whistled around him. Suddenly, he realized that something other than the wind was doing the moaning. He quickened his steps trying to locate the source of the sound that he felt sure was his Delilah.

Finally, after struggling against the elements for another quarter mile, Josiah came upon his missing bovine. The great brown beast was lying on her side, alternately panting and moaning. When she saw Josiah, she raised her head and let out with a tremendous bellow as if pleading for Josiah to help her.

Josiah went round to the business end of things and immediately understood Delilah's distress. Calves are born head first with their heads resting on their front hooves. The muzzle of the calf was showing, but only one hoof could be seen. The second hoof must be caught in the birth canal. Josiah, who had grown up on a dairy farm in England, knew that Delilah would need help to birth her calf safely. Carefully, so as to cause Delilah as little discomfort as possible, Josiah inserted his hand into the birth canal, feeling gently for the other hoof. Yes, there it was, bent underneath the calf's leg. Gently, slowly, Josiah manipulated the little foot as he had seen his father do many times before, until the leg was fully extended.

By now, though, Delilah was exhausted from her efforts and Josiah knew that she was going to need more help. As the little calf bleated its distress, Josiah tied the rope he had brought securely around the two hooves. Using all his strength he began gently to pull the calf out. Because Delilah was unable to help in the process, this took enormous effort on Josiah's part. He grunted loudly under the strain, all the while talking softly to Delilah, assuring her that all would be well. At first, the calf did not move at all, but just as Josiah was beginning to fear the worst, he felt a slight movement and redoubled his efforts. Slowly, the calf emerged and in a rush of fluid, the new life came sliding into a world of crashing thunder and blinding lightning. Delilah bellowed loudly and raised her tired head to look behind her to see her new baby.

Josiah knew that the baby needed to be cleaned and dried quickly or it might not survive. Normally, the mother would do this, but Delilah was clearly exhausted from her ordeal. Josiah sensed that, though willing, the new mother might not be able to fulfill her duties. It was left to Josiah to get the mother and the calf back to his homestead before the damage was done. He tried to get Delilah to stand, but she seemed uninterested. Josiah blew out the lantern. He would come back for it tomorrow. Kneeling by the calf and grabbing two legs in each hand, he hoisted the calf onto his back, head under one arm, tail under the other, and struggled to his feet. He walked in front of Delilah so she could see that he had her calf and began heading back through the dune grass. Delilah gave a great bellow of concern, heaved herself to her feet, and began to plod slowly after Josiah and her calf.

The storm had intensified greatly during the birthing, and without his lantern to light his way, Josiah became somewhat disoriented. He walked steadily for a time. As a great flash of lightning illuminated the landscape, he was surprised to see the beach ahead of him and to hear the crashing surf that always came with these great storms. Thinking that it might be easier to walk along the beach than trying to wade through the sodden beach brass, Josiah started forward again, but stopped when the next flash of lightning revealed a large ship just offshore. Stranger still was the next image revealed to him. A small dinghy was being rowed ashore by two men while a third sat in the stern, evidently shouting orders.

Now ordinarily, Josiah's first instinct would have been to offer assistance to the imperiled boat, but Josiah did not move forward. Indeed, he stepped back into the grass and crouched as low as he could while maintaining his view of the beach. What had stopped him from his natural inclination to help was the appearance of the men in the boat. They were certainly sailors, but not the ordinary sort. No, this was clearly a trio of cutthroats. Pirates!

Josiah hunkered down into the grass, covering the baby calf with beach grass to keep it warm. Delilah began to lick the calf's head, cleaning it of the birth fluid. Josiah kept watch and saw the dinghy come aground on the shore. The leader of the band issued more orders, and the two underlings lifted a heavy chest from the small boat and struggled across the beach with it. They stopped beside one of the huge bluestone boulders which dotted the shore and returned to the boat for shovels. Hurrying back to the chest, they began to dig, clearly planning to bury the chest.

Some minutes later, a hole large enough to accommodate the chest had been dug. Apparently the leader of the gang was not satisfied, and the two men began digging again until the hole had been enlarged considerably. They heaved and dragged the chest until it slipped into the hole and picked up their shovels to finish the task. It was then that things took an ominous turn. Suddenly the leader of the trio pulled a brace of pistols from his belt and without a moment's hesitation, shot both men. Despite the racket from the storm, the sound of the guns was very loud and Delilah gave a great bellow.

Josiah whispered harshly to Delilah, "Hush your noise, you foolish cow! Would you get us both killed?"

The pirate, clearly sensing a new sound, looked suspiciously in all directions. His gaze swept over the place where Josiah hid. Josiah held his breath.

Apparently satisfied that all was well, the pirate pushed his compatriots into the hole, picked up one of the shovels and filled in the hole.

Josiah was shaking from both fear and cold, but he was afraid to stir until the pirate returned to the dinghy and began rowing back to the mother ship. Josiah waited until the dinghy swung-to on the seaward side of the ship. Then, sure that in the dark he could not be seen, he picked up the little calf, urged Delilah to her feet, and headed home.

Sometime later, Delilah and her calf were safely back in the barn. Josiah began to vigorously wipe dry the little calf until Delilah nosed him away and began to do the job of mothering. The little calf tottered on spindly legs and without too much guidance found the udders filled with its mother's milk. Taking this as a good sign, Josiah returned to the house and settled in front of a warm fire with a mug of hot cider and proceeded to tell his young wife his amazing tale of adventure.

1

"Dad, do we really have to leave today?"

"'Fraid so, kiddo. School starts on Thursday, and I have to get back to work."

"School! Why does it always have to ruin everything?"

Andy Bennett kicked at a stone in the road as he and his father, Ben, meandered along the edge of the bluff. Nantucket Sound was quiet as a mill pond. It was what his mother, Rachel, called a perfect Vineyard day. "Blue and gold" she would say. Andy always thought the water looked as if a fairy had sprinkled gold glitter all over it. It was so bright, it almost hurt his eyes.

"Hey, wait for me!" cried Andy's twin sister, Samantha, better known as Sam. Pounding along the bluff road, she raced to catch up to Andy and their dad.

"Mom says we should stop and say goodbye to Mrs. Harrington," gasped Sam as she tried to get her breath.

"That's a good idea," agreed their dad. "This is probably the last time we'll see her."

"Why?" asked Sam with a note of panic in her voice. "Aren't we coming back to the Vineyard next summer?"

"Sure we are. But Mrs. Harrington is moving to North Carolina to live with her daughter and her family. She's selling *Windswept*."

"Wow—maybe we can we buy it, Dad!" said Andy.

"Yeah!" agreed Sam. "That would be cool. Then we could come whenever we wanted, instead of only renting a house for a month!"

"I admit it would be nice to have a place here, but I'm afraid it would be a little out of our budget!"

"Maybe she'll sell it to us cheap because we're such adorable children," laughed Sam.

"Right!" scoffed Ben. "More likely she'd raise the price!"

"There's nothing like the loving support of a parent," chided Andy.

"And nothing like twins ganging up on their poor father!" retorted Ben.

They were all laughing as they approached Mrs. Harrington's house. A carved sign proclaiming the house's name, *Windswept*, hung above a lovely wide front porch that overlooked the sea. As with many Vineyard houses built in the Victorian style, atop *Windswept* was a small tower which added to the character of the house. White wicker chairs with blue flowered cushions and a porch swing made an inviting scene. Sam and Andy had spent many enjoyable afternoons on this porch, sipping ice cold lemonade and eating some of Mrs. Harrington's famous molasses cookies. The walk leading to the house was planted with colorful zinnias and even now, in early September, their red and yellow blossoms offered a colorful welcome to visitors.

As they approached the front steps, an elderly woman with almost pure white hair, wearing a pale yellow dress printed with seashells, came out onto the porch.

"Hi, Mrs. Harrington!" shouted Sam as she raced up the porch steps.

"Sam, what a nice surprise. Isn't this a beautiful day?"

"It is," agreed Sam. "Except for the fact that Dad just told us you were moving away from the Vineyard."

"Yes, I am," replied Mrs. Harrington in a melancholy tone. "I don't want to, but I think it's probably the best thing."

"I would never leave the Vineyard if I didn't have to!" cried Andy.

"Neither would I!" agreed Mrs. Harrington. "Hello, Ben. How nice of you to visit. Where's Rachel?"

"Home—cleaning. You know Rachel. She's determined to leave that house twice as clean as she found it. Em Michaels says she would like to clone Rachel and only rent to her."

"I don't blame her. Poor Em is completely exhausted from dealing with all the renters she had this summer. That's why I'm going to sell my house instead of renting it. I don't want the worry. Besides, there's a lot of upkeep with these old houses."

"I can imagine. Still, they don't build them with this kind of character anymore."

"That's true," replied Mrs. Harrington.

"Mrs. Harrington, can I ask you something?" inquired Andy.

"Of course, Andy. What?"

"Well, I was wondering—what's in the tower?"

Mrs. Harrington's eyes widened and she took a very deep breath. Andy thought she looked kind of scared.

"I can't tell you, Andy."

"How come?" Andy whispered, a bit of afraid of what she was going to say.

"Because," she paused, "I don't know."

"You've never been up there?" asked Sam.

"No, Sam. Never."

"Why not?"

"Well, one day when I was about your age, I decided to climb up and see what was in the tower. I was just about to push open the trap door when my father called me down. He was—well, not exactly angry, but he was very stern with me. He told me that I was never to go into the tower. I asked him why, but he just said it was for my own good."

"So you never did?" asked Andy.

"Well, I did try a few weeks later, but when I got to the top of the stairs—" Mrs. Harrington stopped.

"What?" cried Sam.

"I heard something over my head. I don't know what it was. I might have been overly sensitive after my father's warning, but it really frightened me. I tumbled down the stairs right into my father. He was very angry with me for disobeying his orders. Right after that, he padlocked the trap door and I never climbed those steps again."

"Wow, so you never found out what the noise was?" asked Sam.

"No," admitted Mrs. Harrington in an eerily quiet voice.

"Did you ever hear it again?" asked Andy

"I'm not sure, but one night during a bad thunderstorm I would swear I heard moaning coming from the tower. My mother told me it was my imagination. And I'm sure it was. You know how children are."

"I certainly do," agreed Ben, giving Sam and Andy a knowing look.

"Oh, I am going to miss the old girl. I just hope someone nice comes along to buy her. I feel as if I'm selling one of my own children!"

"Hey, Mrs. Harrington—do you have any cookies?" asked Andy.

"Andy!" exclaimed his father. "We came to say goodbye to Mrs. Harrington, not to eat her out of house and home! Besides, we have to get back. We're on the two-thirty boat, and we haven't even packed the car yet."

"Dad, it's ten-thirty. I think there's time enough to pack the car *and* have a cookie!" argued Sam.

"I agree with Samantha," said Mrs. Harrington. "I'll get some. And how about some lemonade?"

"Yum!" exclaimed the twins together.

"I guess I'm outnumbered!" surrendered Ben. As he took a seat in one of the wicker chairs, the twins plopped onto the swing and high-fived each other.

They sat in companionable silence until Mrs. Harrington re-emerged through the screen door, letting it slap shut behind her. She carried a tray with a pitcher of lemonade, four glasses, and a plate mounded with cookies. She placed the tray on a low table in front of Ben and poured two glasses from the frosty pitcher. Sam and Andy jumped off the swing and each retrieved a glass of lemonade and a cookie. Mrs. Harrington poured lemonade for herself and Ben and offered him the plate of cookies. Taking one he exclaimed, "Wow, they're still warm!"

"I'm trying to use up all the food in my kitchen before I leave."

"When *do* you leave?" asked Andy.

"The nine-thirty boat tomorrow."

"But I thought you had to sell your house?" cried Sam.

"Em will handle it for me. I'm selling it furnished. Anything I wanted to keep has already been shipped off to North Carolina."

"Well, the island won't be the same without you, Millie," asserted Ben.

"Oh, stuff and nonsense, Ben. The water will close over very quickly."

"Well, we're certainly going to miss you. You've been a wonderful neighbor to us all these summers," insisted Ben.

"Yeah—and Mom never bakes cookies," said Andy with a grin.

"Andrew Jason Bennett!" Ben scolded gently. "Come along you two, while Mrs. Harrington still thinks fondly of you!"

"Come and give me a big hug. It's going to have to last me awhile!" exclaimed Mrs. Harrington. She had tears in her eyes as the twins threw their arms around her and squeezed her hard.

"We're really going to miss you, Mrs. H. Can we write to you?" asked Sam.

"Oh, I would love that. I'm going to keep my subscription to the Gazette, so I can keep track of all the island doings, but I would love to have a private source for all the neighborhood details!" she laughed. "I'll leave my address with Em Michaels. Now, Ben, you'd best give me a hug, too. And give my love to Rachel in case I don't have the chance to see her before you go." Ben went to the older woman and put his arms around her, kissing her on the cheek.

"We'll drive by and honk on our way to the boat," promised Ben. The three headed down the steps and continued along the bluff road toward their own rented cottage. They stopped at the bend in the road to wave again to Mrs. Harrington. She was waving a handkerchief which she occasionally used to dab at her eyes.

2

As they rounded the bend, losing sight of Windswept, Andy exclaimed, "Gee, I wonder who will buy the house. They won't be as nice as Mrs. Harrington!"

"Maybe they'll have kids our age," suggested Sam hopefully.

"That's good positive thinking, Sam."

"Oh Dad—you and your positive thinking," scoffed Andy.

"Nothing wrong with trying to find the positive angle on a difficult situation, son."

With that, they arrived at the little cottage the family had rented since the twins were three years old. It was a simple, one story house with three small bedrooms, a tiny kitchen, and a living room. It was a typical summer house. You could see all the framing studs on the inside. The walls were dark and there was a big, beach stone fireplace at one end of the living room. On cold, blowy, damp days, Ben would make a fire and they would play board games on a rickety old card table. A long narrow porch ran the length of the house. From the porch you could see the bluff road with the water beyond. Sam and Andy thought it was the perfect house.

As they approached, they saw Rachel on the porch beating the living room rug with an old fashioned rug beater. Great clouds of sandy grit flew into the air, and Rachel sneezed loudly several times. Ben rushed ahead of the children and up onto the porch. He grabbed the rug beater away from Rachel with a look of concern on his face.

"For Heaven's sake, Rach, what are you doing? I told you I would beat the rug. This is just going to aggravate your asthma."

"Aaah-choo!" she sneezed. Wiping her nose with a tissue she said, "My hero! But you were gone for so long and I needed to get this done. You need to go down to the post office and check the box one last time."

"Can we go, Dad?" asked Andy.

"Please!" added Sam.

"I'm sure your mother could use some help with the packing," Ben replied.

"Actually, it's probably easier to do it myself. Go ahead and take them. Besides, I'm sure they'd like one last visit to *The Flying Horses*."

"Would we!" cried Sam.

The Flying Horses, in downtown Oak Bluffs, was said to be the oldest continuously operating carousel in the United States. Now, it was owned by the Martha's Vineyard Preservation Trust and was a favorite place for every child on the island.

The three piled into the car and headed down the hill and around the corner by the Beach Club. They passed the harbor that was beginning to empty as Labor Day approached. Knowing that Oak Bluffs' main street, Circuit Avenue, would be crowded with cars, Ben continued on and found a space on Ocean Park. The park was one of the twins' favorite places in Oak Bluffs. It was surrounded by magnificent old Victorian houses and featured a duck pond and a charming bandstand.

Handing each child a dollar, Ben said, "One ride, period. If you get the brass ring, you'll have to save the free ride for next year. Meet me at the Post Office when you're done."

"Thanks, Dad!" cried the twins as they ran for the steep steps that lead up to the carousel house.

As they entered, they heard the electronic sounds of the arcade games and the squeals of a toddler riding the space ship that they had ridden when they were smaller. They could smell the popcorn and hear the music of the merry-go-round's calliope. As they passed through into the larger space where the carousel was housed, they saw the line of waiting children snaking back and forth.

"Come on, we better get the tickets," advised Andy. "We're going to have to wait."

It took nearly twenty minutes for the twins to reach the front of the line. As soon as the spinning horses stopped, the twins made a mad dash for their favorites. Sam chose a caramel colored horse with a wild look in its glass eyes and Andy picked a big black horse.

As soon as the last horse had its rider, the big brass bell was rung and the carousel began to turn, slowly at first and then faster and faster. An older man took the tickets, and a young boy standing on steps to one side of the ride, swung an old wooden cradle of rings into place. The riders reached out in front to grab as many as they could. Most could only catch one, but some old pros could catch two, three, or even four. Sam loved the clicking sound of the rings being pulled from the arm. She was content with one ring each time she went by, but Andy was convinced that the more rings you caught, the better your chances of getting the brass ring which would earn a free ride.

Finally, they heard the announcement, "The brass ring is in the arm!" As the carousel continued to spin, the delicious anticipation began to build. As the riders flew past the arm, they would grab for the rings, eagerly examining their prize to see if one was the coveted brass ring. If not, they would watch behind them to see if someone else had found it.

On the next time around Sam watched the rings slip from the arm into the hands of the riders ahead of her. One girl with a long braid caught three and a little boy in a plaid shirt got two. Still no brass ring had appeared. Just two more kids in front of her.

"Get ready!" she warned herself.

The next boy, a tall skinny kid in a Grateful Dead T-shirt, grabbed four rings and then, glinting in the lights of the carousel, the brass ring. The little

girl in front of her reached out and grabbed for it, pulling it part way out of the cradle, but her little fingers could not pull hard enough to gain the prize. Sam reached for it and it came away easily in her hand. Sam laughed and waved the brass ring at Andy.

"Congratulations," said the man who had taken their tickets.

"Thanks," said Sam. Then she saw the little girl in front of her—tears running down her cheeks. She swallowed hard. "But the little girl in front of me—" Sam stopped. "Please, give it to her."

"That's a nice thing to do," said the man. "Okay. If that's the way you want it."

"It is," replied Sam with more cheer in her voice than she felt. Why was it so hard to do the nice thing?

The man carefully negotiated his way forward to the little girl and handed her the ticket. Sam could tell he was explaining that Sam had wanted her to have it. The little girl turned, smiled and mouthed the words "Thank you". Sam gave her a "thumbs up". As the ride slowed to a stop, Sam swung her leg over the horse and prepared to leave the platform where the wonderful old horses were forever corralled. Just as she was about to get off, the ticket man tapped her on the shoulder.

"Here," he said, holding out a merry-go-round ticket. "That was a real nice thing you did. Have another ride on the Flying Horses."

"Gee, thanks," said Sam, "but my dad said we had to save an extra ride for next summer. Is that okay?"

"Sure. Good for life!" smiled the man. "See you next summer!"

"Gosh, we've been here a half hour!" exclaimed Andy as he joined Sam at the exit from the merry-go-round. "Dad's going to murder us! We'd better run."

Off they ran up Circuit Avenue, past the smell of fried clams at Giordano's and past Mad Martha's Ice Cream to the little plaza onto which the post office faced. They pushed through the doors and looked around for their father. He wasn't at their mail box, or at the service window. They looked around the corner, where the newer boxes were, but he wasn't there either.

"Maybe he came looking for us at the merry-go-round," suggested Andy.

"Well, let's go see," replied Sam as the two exited the post office and turned back toward Circuit Avenue. Just then, they saw their father coming out of the bakery next door. He was carrying a bag and a cup of coffee and talking

to a gray haired lady with a green yarn bow tied around her hair. It was their friend Em Michaels.

"Hi, Aunt Em!" cried the twins. The twins had always called old family friends 'Aunt' or 'Uncle'. For a long time, Andy had thought his parents had dozens of brothers and sisters! "Gee, Dad, we thought we'd lost you!" teased Sam.

"Very funny. You were gone so long, I got hungry. I went in to get a hermit bar and a cup of coffee and ran into Em.

"Is that what's in the bag? Hermit bars?" asked Andy hopefully. He especially liked hermit bars.

"Actually, no. It's an éclair for your mother, since she's at home working while we ride merry-go-rounds and eat cookies."

"Seems fair to me," put in Em.

"Aunt Em! Whose side are you on?" demanded Andy.

"I never take sides in matters involving baked goods," she laughed.

"Have a good winter, Em. And thanks for your help."

"No problem. I'll be in touch." Ben gave Em a kiss on the cheek and as she headed into the post office, Ben and the twins returned to their car on the park.

"What did Aunt Em help you with, Dad?" asked Sam.

"None of your business," retorted Ben. "Now let's get a wiggle on or we'll miss that boat!"

3

They'd been home for over a week. School had started the previous Thursday. Andy was already studying for a math test. How could life change so quickly?

"Andy, will you stop day dreaming," pleaded his mother. "The rest of us are waiting to have dessert!"

"Sorry," he apologized as he shoveled the last forkful of meat loaf into his mouth and stood to clear the plates, which was his job.

"So, I'm going in early tomorrow in order to be ready for our big date," said Ben.

"You're a nut!" said Rachel smiling at Ben.

"What's nutty about dinner out on the town to celebrate our fifteenth wedding anniversary? I think fifteen years of 'happily married' is pretty special!"

"I do, too," cried Sam. "Wow, fifteen years. You've been married more years than I've been alive."

"I certainly hope so," laughed Rachel.

• • •

"You have ten minutes left," announced Mrs. Riefler the next morning as Andy erased his answer for the fourth time. Who needed to know how to divide anyway? He worked the problem again and finally got it to check. As he was reviewing his work, there was a knock on the door and Mrs. Bankos, the principal, came into the room. She motioned to Mrs. Riefler to join her in the hall. When Mrs. Riefler returned, Andy thought she looked sort of sick.

"Boys and girls, would you put your pencils down please and join me in Open Circle?"

"But I'm not done," whined Kelly Fisher.

"I know, Kelly. Don't worry about it. We'll finish later. Just come to Open Circle now, please."

As they had done since kindergarten, the children quietly but quickly moved their chairs into a circle and sat down. Each child took the hand of the classmate on either side and raised their hands over their heads saying, "Circle is open."

Mrs. Riefler looked very serious as she began to speak, and Andy got a scary feeling that she was going to say something awful.

"Children, as fifth graders, you are old enough to know that we live in a world where bad things happen. Sometimes they are simply accidents or acts of nature about which we can do very little. Sometimes, though, bad people do bad things. I'm afraid that's what has happened today."

The children exchanged wondering looks as Mrs. Riefler went on.

"This morning, in New York City, some very bad people flew jet airplanes into the World Trade Center."

Andy felt his stomach lurch. His father's office was in the World Trade Center.

"Were people hurt, Mrs. Riefler?" he asked hesitantly.

"Yes, I'm afraid some people were hurt, Andy. We don't know any details yet."

"Mrs. Riefler, my dad works in the World Trade Center."

"Yes, I know Andy. We've called your mom, and she's on her way. I'm sorry, we don't know anything more."

Just then, the door to the classroom opened and Sam came in. She ran to her brother.

"Andy, we have to go home. Dad's office—"

"I know. Mom's coming. It'll be okay, Sam." He turned to his teacher. "Can I go, Mrs. Riefler?"

"Of course, Andy. We'll be thinking of you and saying prayers."

"Thanks."

He took his sister's hand and led her out of the classroom. Mrs. Bankos was waiting for them, and she took them down the hall to the main office. They saw their mom come through the front door and they ran to her. She dropped to her knees and opened her arms, gathering in her children.

"Mom!" cried Sam. "Is Dad okay?"

"I don't know. I was at the grocery store. School called me on my cell. I didn't even know it had happened. I'm sure he's okay. Let's go home. There's probably a message from him telling us he's fine," she said with more confidence than she felt.

She led the children to her car which was parked out front of the school, and they drove the two blocks to their home. As they opened the front door, they all looked at the answering machine. A red light was flashing.

4

"See, I told you," said Rachel as she reached for the button that would play back the message.

"You have one message," said the mechanical voice. "First message, received today at nine-o-one."

"Hi, Rach." They cheered as they heard their father's voice.

"Honey, something bad has happened here. I'm not sure what it is, but some sort of explosion. Someone said it was a plane. It's somewhere below us, but I don't know exactly where. There's a lot of smoke. I'm not—oh my God—the South Tower just got hit. I can't believe this. A plane flew right into the South Tower. Rach, this is bad. Tim Fuller is leading a group up to the roof since we can't go down. I don't know what's going to happen, Rach. I may not make our date tonight."

They could hear tears in his voice as he finished the call.

"Sam, Andy—if anything happens and I don't get home, take care of your Mom and each other. I love you more than—" and the message abruptly ended.

"Mom?" asked Andy fearfully.

"I don't know. Probably the phone lines just went dead. That often happens in these situations. You heard him. He's okay and he's going up to the roof. I'm sure they'll send helicopters to rescue them."

Just then Sam walked into the hall. "Mom?"

Rachel took one look at her daughter's face and knew something terrible had happened.

"What is it, Sam?" asked Rachel, not really wanting to hear the answer.

"It fell down."

"What fell down, honey?" Rachel could not grasp the meaning of Sam's statement.

"The tower."

"What are you talking about?" laughed Andy nervously. "You're telling me the World Trade Center fell down? That's impossible."

"I—I know," stuttered Sam, "but it did. Just like some kind of kid's toy.

It just—oh, Mom," wailed Sam as she burst into tears, "what's happened to Daddy?"

Trying to stay calm, Rachel replied, "I don't know, sweetheart. I imagine it will be quite awhile before we know anything. Until then, we're going to—"

"Have a positive attitude!" both children said in unison and actually laughed through their tears as they echoed the philosophy that had always guided their father's life.

"That's right." Just then the phone rang. Rachel grabbed for it like a drowning woman reaching for a life preserver. "Ben?" she almost screamed into the phone, but her shoulders sagged as she heard the voice of Ben's mother.

"No, Rachel dear, it's Eleanor. I guess you've answered my question without my asking it. You haven't heard from Ben?"

"There was a message on the machine. I was out at the store. I got a call from school and went and got the kids. I don't know—the call just ended. Oh my God—what are we going to do?" cried Rachel as the dam broke and the fear and the anguish she had been holding in overwhelmed her. She slid down the wall, her shaking hands still holding the receiver, and sobbed. Sam and Andy had never seen their mother so upset, and it frightened them.

"Mom!" cried Sam. "It'll be okay. Dad will be all right. He has to be." She gently pried the receiver from Rachel's hand and spoke to her grandmother.

"Gommy, I don't know what to do. Mom is crying so hard. I'm scared, Gommy."

"I know you are, darling. Gompy and I are on our way. We'll be there in a few minutes. Try and get your mother to calm down. Can you make her some tea?"

"Yeah, I can do that. Gommy, the tower fell down."

"Yes, honey, I know. It's terrible—awful. Try to hang on, Sam. We'll be there as fast as we can."

"Okay, Gommy," responded Sam and hung up the phone. She gave Andy a serious, grownup look as she reached down for her mother whose sobs had quieted.

"Come on, Mom. Gommy and Gompy are coming. I'm going to make you some tea."

As if their mother was suddenly the child and they the parents, the twins pulled Rachel to her feet and took her into the kitchen. They sat her down at the old kitchen table and Sam put the kettle on. She got out Rachel's favorite blue teapot and the pretty blue and white flowered cups that Rachel had inherited from her mother. When Rachel saw the cups, the tears returned. Her mother had only died two years ago and she still missed her so much. Now, she felt the loss more than ever, longing for her mother's comforting hugs and good advice. She knew in her heart that Ben was not going to come home that night or ever again.

"My Ben—my Ben," she murmured over and over as tears coursed down her cheeks and fell in a puddle onto the kitchen table. Eventually, the tea kettle whistled and Sam made the tea. She was just pouring it when her grandparents arrived.

"Gompy, Mom just sits there crying, saying 'my Ben' over and over."

"It's all right," comforted their grandfather, a gentle kind man whose own heart was breaking at the thought of losing his only child. "She'll be all right. Why don't you young folks go upstairs and get out of your school clothes and then we'll see about some lunch."

"I'm not hungry," said Andy. Sam looked at him with grave concern. She had never heard those words from Andy before.

"Never mind—you'll eat something anyway," said Gommy. "You're going to need all your strength to get through this. Now, do as Gompy said and go get changed."

The twins started out of the kitchen, and then Sam turned back and gave both her grandparents a hug. Gently, she took Andy's hand and led him up the stairs to their bedrooms to change.

5

The next days were just a blur for all of them. After the first few hours they turned off the television. They couldn't stand to watch, knowing that somewhere in the rubble of the giant towers lay the broken body of their father, their husband, their son.

Neighbors brought food constantly, but no one ate much, despite Gommy's urging.

They didn't remember much about the memorial service for their father. There had been music and lots of flowers. Ben had coached Andy's baseball team and Sam's soccer team. All the players had come to the service. Mrs. Riefler and Sam's teacher, Mr. Montick, had brought their entire classes to the little church that was right across the street from the school. All their classmates made cards and wrote poems.

Afterwards, back at their house, everyone had eaten sandwiches and cookies and talked about Ben and how great he was. By four o'clock their guests had gone home and Rachel had gone to lie down. Sam and Andy were sitting in the living room with Gommy and Gompy.

"Gommy, I'm worried about Mom. Her eyes—they're sort of—dead looking. When I talk to her, it's as if she's not there."

"I know, Sam. Try to understand. Your mother's life has fallen apart. You still have your mom, the person you can depend upon, but your mom has lost that person. She feels very alone right now."

"But we're here," cried Andy. "Don't we count?"

"Of course you do," assured Gompy. "Why if it weren't for you two, I don't think your Mom would have made it through these last few days. She loves you guys with all her heart. You're going to have to be very patient and gentle with her for the next little while until she figures out how to handle all this."

"We will be, Gompy," promised Sam and Andy together.

"We know you will," said Gommy.

And they were. For the next few weeks, the twins took on most of the household chores. They answered the phone and took careful messages because

Rachel couldn't talk to people without crying. She spent a lot of time in bed, sleeping late into the morning, so the twins had to get their own breakfast and get themselves to school. Often, when they came home in the afternoon, they would find a note from their mother saying she was napping and please not to disturb her.

Their grandparents called every day and came by several times a week. They were concerned, too.

"I hear her wandering around the house at night," admitted Sam one day. "I think that's why she sleeps so much during the day."

"You're probably right," agreed her grandfather. "Still, I think she needs to try to get back into some sort of a routine. I'm going up to speak to her."

He was gone for quite awhile, but when he came down, Rachel was with him. She had put on a dress and combed her hair for the first time in weeks. She sat down on the sofa and patted the spaces on either side of her, indicating that Sam and Andy should join her.

"You guys," she said smiling and ruffling their hair. "What would I do without you? Your daddy would have been so proud of you, the way you've taken up the slack these past weeks. I'm sorry that I deserted you. I guess I was just scared and confused."

"Are you better now?" asked Andy.

Rachel looked lovingly at her father-in-law and smiled as she said, "Yes. Better. Not all well yet, but definitely better." She paused. "Now, we're going to have to make some decisions and some changes. See, I have been thinking all this time, trying to figure things out. Our lives are going to change as a result of this. I thought I had to make all the decisions and that scared me, but Gompy helped me realize that you guys need to be part of the decision making process too, since it's going to affect your lives as much as mine."

"What kind of decisions?" asked Sam.

"Well, the big one is this house."

"What about the house?"

"Well, I'm not sure we can afford it without Dad's salary. There's the mortgage payment and the taxes are high. I'm afraid we may have to move to another area where it's not as expensive to live."

"You mean like a whole other town?" asked Andy, horrified at the thought of leaving his school and his friends.

"I'm afraid so. I've talked to Mr. Littlefield, our accountant, and he says there's no way around it. He says we may get some sort of settlement from the government, but there's no telling how much that will be or when we'll get it, so we have to assume the worst."

"But Dad always said to have a positive attitude!" protested Sam.

"I know. And in this case, I think he would say that making choices now, while we can have a little time to decide what we want, is better than waiting until we are forced to take whatever is available."

"But I don't want to move," wailed Andy.

"I don't either, but we may have to, so we might as well make an adventure of it. Now, I have a lot of mail to catch up on. I'm sure there are tons of notes that need to be answered."

"I hope you don't mind," interrupted Gommy, "I answered all the ones from people that Gompy and I knew and from friends of yours and Ben's that we had met."

"Bless your heart, Gommy. How can I thank you? I was dreading it, and I know it can't have been easy for you."

"No, it wasn't," she said sadly, "but it was comforting to read all the wonderful things people had to say about Ben. We always thought he was a fine young man, but it helps to hear other people say it. I've saved them all for you, of course, and when you're ready, I hope you'll read them. They are as much a testament to you and the love you and Ben shared as anything else."

They sat in silence for a few minutes and then Andy said, "Oh Mom, there was a Fed Ex for you a few days ago, too."

"Probably something from Mr. Littlefield. He said he was going to send me some papers to sign. Will you get it for me, kiddo?"

"Sure!"

In a moment, Andy was back with the cardboard envelope. He was reading the label and looking puzzled.

"It's not from Mr. Littlefield," he announced. "It's from Aunt Em at the Vineyard."

"Oh gosh—probably a bunch of notes from Vineyard people," suggested Rachel opening the envelope and extracting a sheaf of papers with a letter clipped to the top. Rachel began to read the letter to herself and as she did, her hands began to shake so hard that she almost dropped the packet.

"Mom, what is it?" asked Sam, alarmed.

"Listen," said Rachel and then she read:

"My dearest Rachel, Andy and Sam,

This is such a difficult letter to write, knowing the terrible loss you are trying to come to grips with. First, please know that everyone here is holding you in their hearts and keeping you in their prayers. We had a little impromptu service for Ben here at the lighthouse and when you are ready, there is a videotape of it for you to see.

The reason for this letter, however, is that before Ben died, in fact the last day he was here on the island, he bought you an anniversary present, Rachel.

Given the circumstances now, I'm not sure how it will be received, but he wanted you to have it, so I'm doing my part.

As you know, Millie Harrington moved to North Carolina to live with her children. She decided to sell her house, Windswept. Ben bought it for you, Rachel."

Rachel stopped. The tears were back and she found it difficult to go on. She took a deep breath and continued.

"He said that the happiest times you spent as a family were here on the island, and he knew how much you and the kids wanted a house here where you could stay as long as you wanted. He told me that you and the children were the greatest gift God ever gave him, and he wanted to do something special to show you how much he loved all of you.

When Millie learned of his desire to buy the house, she was thrilled and offered it to Ben at a very good price, so the deal was made.

The house is yours with a small mortgage. It is of course a summer house. No heat, although Millie often stayed there well into December using the wood stove to heat the house quite effectively. It's also furnished with what Millie called "genteel shabby" furniture.

Rachel, I don't know what you will decide about the house, but if I can be of any help, please don't hesitate to call me. My heart aches for all of you. Love, Em"

Rachel let the letter fall into her lap. "How typical! What a nut case. A house on the Vineyard," she began to laugh. "If there's one thing I don't need right now, it's another house. I guess we can sell it and use it to help finance a new place."

"Sell it?" Andy shouted, astonished. "How could you sell it? We've always wanted a house on the Vineyard and it was Dad's last gift to us. It's like all the love he had for us is in that house. You can't sell it!" Andy was on the verge of tears.

"Andy, I just got through explaining to you that we can't even afford this house, never mind the expense and upkeep of a summer house. I know Dad wanted us to have it, but I'm sure he would agree with me that it just isn't possible."

"But, Mom," Sam interrupted, "if we have to move anyway, why don't we—why couldn't we move to the Vineyard? They have schools there. And Aunt Em said there was only a small mortgage. If we sell this house, we could use the money to finish paying for *Windswept*."

"Don't be ridiculous. People don't live at the Vineyard."

"Aunt Em does," retorted Sam.

"Well, besides, it's a summer house. There's no heat. And I have to get a job. What kind of job could I get at the Vineyard? It's impractical and impossible and—" she burst into tears.

"Mom!" cried Andy. "Don't cry. It's okay. We understand. If you don't want to keep the house, it's okay. I'm sure we'll find a nice house somewhere."

"That's just it—I do want to keep it. You're right. It was the last gift your Dad gave us. How can I not keep it?"

"Rachel, dear," began Gompy.

"Don't say it—I know. It doesn't make any sense. But maybe I can use the money from this house to renovate *Windswept* and make it livable."

"But what about a job? Unemployment is awfully high on the island, isn't it?"

"Well, I'm not exactly a hot property here either. I haven't worked in fifteen years. Wherever I end up, it's not going to be easy getting a job."

"Yes, but there are more opportunities here," protested Gommy.

"Mom, please!" begged Sam and Andy.

"Rachel, you have to be sensible," cautioned Gompy.

There was a long pause. Then Rachel asked, "Why?"

"What do you mean, 'why'?" asked Gompy.

"Is there anything sensible about this? Where is the sense in a bunch of fanatics hijacking a jet and flying it into an office tower? Where is the sense in a wonderful man like Ben having his life cut short by such senseless violence? Where is the sense in my children growing up without a father? There is no sense in any of it. So why do we have to be sensible now? The kids want it—I want it. I want to be where we were happiest. I want to be able to wake up and see the ocean, walk on the beach and look for sea glass, be where his spirit is. It may not be sensible to you, but it makes perfect sense to me."

"But we'll never see you!" cried Gommy.

"Of course you will," protested Rachel. "You will come and visit us, and we'll come to visit you."

"It won't be the same," said Gompy.

"Gompy," said Sam, "nothing will ever be the same again, no matter where we live."

For the first time since her dad had died, Sam saw tears in Gompy's eyes. Rachel went to her father-in-law and took his hand in hers.

"Gompy, I'm sorry. For a moment, we seemed to forget that you and Gommy lost Ben, too."

"You're not supposed to bury your children," whispered Gompy tearfully. "I don't want to lose you, too."

"Gompy, there's no way you could lose us," Rachel reassured the older man. "Any more than we can ever really lose Ben. He's right here," she said pointing to her heart. "He's right next to you and Gommy and my mom and dad. Sure we might have to work a little harder to actually spend time with each other, but maybe that's a good thing. If this whole nightmare has taught me one thing, it's not to take people and relationships for granted. I'll tell you what, let's plan to have Thanksgiving at the Vineyard. I'll call Em and ask her to open the house and lay in some firewood for the stove. We can bring all the food with us and have a long weekend in the house. After that, we can see how we feel and decide what we want to do. What do you say?"

"Sounds good to me!" cried Andy.

"Me, too," agreed Sam.

Gommy and Gompy exchanged looks.

"That seems very sensible," said Gommy.

6

When the school bell rang at 12:45 on the Wednesday before Thanksgiving, the children poured from the building, shouting with excitement at the prospect of the long holiday weekend ahead. Andy and Sam met their mother at the curb and piled into the family station wagon. Their dad had always refused to buy one of the big gas guzzling SUVs.

Rachel was dressed in jeans and a plaid flannel shirt. She wore fleece lined hiking boots, and there was a bright blue down parka on the back seat with hat, gloves and scarf poking out from the pockets.

"You look like you're heading to the Yukon, Mom," laughed Sam as she settled into the back seat and fastened her seatbelt.

"It was only thirty-five degrees on the island this morning, and we're going to be staying in a drafty house without central heating. Besides, the weather channel said we're going to get a real nor'easter this weekend. Joke if you like, but don't come begging to borrow my warm clothes when you're freezing in your shorts and sandals, or whatever you packed."

"Gosh, Mom, what kind of dumb kids do you think you raised?" asked Andy. "We packed warm stuff. We're just teasing you. And I'm hungry."

"Well, there's a surprise! We'll stop for some burgers before we get on the highway, but I want to get going. The traffic's going to be bad on ninety-five, and we have a boat to catch! Buckle up! Headin' out!" she cried as she put the car in gear and headed for the local fast food restaurant.

A half hour later, happily munching hamburgers, French fries and chocolate milk shakes, they headed for the George Washington Bridge. That would take them to Route 95 north towards New England and their beloved Martha's Vineyard.

"Why didn't Gommy and Gompy come in our car?" asked Andy.

"Well, in the first place, it would be a bit of a tight squeeze. One of you would have had to ride in the way back with the turkey."

"That would mean two turkeys in the way back!" teased Sam.

"Besides it's possible that I may have to stay a little longer."

"Why?" asked Andy.

"Well, if we make some sort of decision—and I'm not saying we will," added Rachel hastily, "but if we do, I'm either going to need to arrange for the sale of the house or start talking to contractors. So I might have to stay longer and, of course," she paused for dramatic effect, "you two have to go back to school!"

Both children groaned.

. . .

By the time they arrived in the little village of Woods Hole, Massachusetts, it was dark and a cold northeast wind was howling. The great bellied ferry was still disgorging the cars and trucks it had transported from the Vineyard as Rachel checked in and maneuvered the car into the line waiting to board for the return trip. A few minutes later, they heard a horn honk and they saw their grandparents' car pull into the lane beside them.

With their tickets checked, the cars slowly snaked toward the great gaping mouth of the ferry. After they were in place, they got out of their cars and climbed the stairs to the seating area. They found two three-seater benches facing each other and settled in for the journey to the Vineyard.

Once the boat left the dock, Rachel and Gommy went up to the lunch counter on the top deck and came back with clam chowder and hotdogs for everyone. After they finished, Gommy opened the duffle she had carried aboard and brought out a plastic box.

"Chocolate chip or peanut butter?" she asked.

"Chocolate chip for me," said Gompy.

"Me, too!" agreed Sam.

"I'll have peanut butter," said Andy. "Thanks for bringing them, Gommy."

"You're welcome. I think I'll have peanut butter, too."

They settled down with their cookies. While the grownups conversed quietly, Sam and Andy stared out the window as the lights of Woods Hole disappeared, and the welcoming beacon of the West Chop lighthouse cut through the night. The harbor at Vineyard Haven is nestled between two spits of land called *chops* and each has its own lighthouse

By the time they disembarked, the wind had been joined by a driving rain, and the predicted nor'easter was in full swing. As they drove the beach road, the waves splashed up over the seawall. A giant puddle that always formed when there was a big storm had already submerged the lower road around East

Chop. As they rounded the corner and started up the hill that would take them past the East Chop lighthouse, Sam listened for the bell buoy that sat offshore. It always seemed to be welcoming them back to the Vineyard.

When they finally pulled into the driveway at *Windswept*, the house was ablaze with lights and smoke was rising from the chimney. Standing in the doorway was Aunt Em, and as they gathered their luggage and trudged up the steps to the side door, she gave them each a hug and a kiss, holding Rachel tightly and whispering to her. When they separated, they both had tears on their cheeks.

"You must have had a long drive. The traffic's always dreadful the day before Thanksgiving," said their old family friend as she followed the tired travelers into the house.

"Ninety-five was jammed from the bridge all the way to New Haven, but once we got through that, it wasn't too bad," responded Rachel. "I sure am glad to be here, though. Thanks for having everything so nice for us, Em. I don't think I could have faced a dark cold house."

She turned to the children. "Okay, you two, bed making time."

"Actually, I made the beds up this afternoon," said Em. Andy and Sam high-fived each other.

"You're the best, Aunt Em," chorused the twins.

"You certainly are. How can I thank you?" added Rachel.

"No thanks are necessary. I'm so glad you're here. It gets a little lonely this time of year. A lot of folks go off island to spend the holiday with family, so it's just us orphans." She laughed, but stopped suddenly as the meaning of what she had said suddenly occurred to her. "Oh my—I'm sorry. I didn't mean that the way it—".

"Of course you didn't, Em," interrupted Rachel. "And we're very grateful to be included in the group. Aren't we kids?"

"Yup."

"Absolutely!"

"Now, we'd better figure out who's sleeping where," she said. "I've never been in the upstairs of this house. I don't even know how many bedrooms there are, Em."

"A lot! There are four bedrooms in the front part of the house and one more in the maids' quarters in the back. Plus, there's a guest suite in the back of the garage."

"Maids' quarters?" cried Sam. "I didn't know Mrs. Harrington had a maid."

"Oh, she didn't," replied Aunt Em, "but when this house was built, many families had live-in help, so separate quarters were included in the design of the houses. Let's go up and you can take a look," she suggested.

The stairs were typical of old Cape Cod houses. They were very steep and twisted sharply after a small landing. At the top of the stairs was a small hallway. In the floor was a metal grate through which you could see down to the first floor. The grate was there so the heat from the stove could rise to warm the second floor. Off the hallway was the bathroom with a big old-fashioned claw footed tub, a toilet with a large water tank hanging above it and an old pedestal sink. Two steps down from this part of the hall was a spacious bedroom. There was a large mahogany bed with a snow white cotton spread. White organdy curtains crisscrossed a beautiful bay window that looked out to the sea.

"This was Millie's room," said Aunt Em.

"Oh, it's lovely," breathed Rachel.

"Hey, look. There's a sink in the room!" cried Andy in surprise.

"Yes, all the rooms have sinks. That was very common when these houses were built. It saves long lines at the bathroom. By the way, there's one full bath here, one in the servants quarters, and a half bath downstairs."

"I think you should have this room, Mom," said Andy.

"Well, what do you know? I agree!" laughed Rachel. She put her suitcase on the luggage rack that sat in one corner and turned back to the group. "Shall we continue the tour?"

"So, the servant's quarters are through those doors," said Em, pointing to a pair of double doors on the far wall of the room. "There's a separate stairway from the kitchen," she said as she led the little party back out into the hall. Two steps up from the bathroom, a long narrow hallway led to three more bedrooms.

The first bedroom was small. There was an old fashioned iron bedstead painted white and covered with a flowered quilt. The walls were painted yellow and the wood floor was painted a rich dark green. The dresser and other furniture pieces were a paler green and a green braided rug covered part of the floor. A small squared off alcove at the far side of the room held a beautiful old

rocking chair and a hand painted toy chest. The windows
water to Cape Cod.

"Oh, can I have this room?" cried Sam the moment sh

"Is that okay with you, Andy?" asked Rachel.

"Definitely! It's too girly for me," he snorted in disgust.

"I think the room across the hall will be perfect for you Andy," said Aunt
Em.

She was right. Andy was delighted with the cream colored room awash
in all things nautical. Model sailing ships, an old leather trunk and a rustic
wooden captain's bed with storage drawers in the base would have been enough,
but the telescope by the window sealed the deal for Andy.

Finally, Em showed Gommy and Gompy a beautiful big room at the end
of the hall. It faced directly onto the sea and had two beautiful antique carved
wooden beds. There were two comfortably overstuffed chairs with a small table
in the little bay window where one could sit and read or look out at the sea.
There were two old painted wooden dressers and two small closets.

"Well, I must say, this is a perfectly charming house," said Gommy. "It
reminds me of a beautiful little inn we stayed in near Newport. Do you remember, dear?" she asked Gompy.

"How could I forget?" exclaimed Gompy. "It was our honeymoon, after
all! The only difference is, when we stayed there, these types of furnishings were
considered modern!" He laughed and Gommy pretended to take a swing at
him.

"What are those stairs?" asked Sam, pointing to an extremely narrow set
of stairs that led up from the hall.

"I bet they go to the tower," suggested Andy.

"I think you're right," agreed Sam.

"Could I have that on tape please—I mean the part about my being
right?" quipped Andy.

"Yeah, right. A once in a lifetime thing!" laughed Sam.

"Well, I say we should find out!" cried Andy as he started for them.

"Hang on there, Christopher Columbus!" laughed Rachel. "You can go
exploring tomorrow. Right now, what do you say we get a good night's sleep?
I'm sure Aunt Em would like to get back to her own house and bed."

"Well, yes, I guess I would," she admitted. "I left flashlights by each bed, se you lose power. We often do in a nor'easter. Luckily the cook stove is propane, so even if you lose power, you can still cook. The fridge is stocked with eggs, bacon, milk and juice, and there's a loaf of bread from the Black Dog Bakery, too. Thanksgiving dinner is at my house tomorrow at four."

"Do you want to take the turkey with you now, Em?" asked Rachel.

"Yes, I guess that would make the most sense. You were so sweet to bring it all this way."

"We wanted to make a contribution and that was a pretty easy one," responded Rachel.

"I brought some nice wine for the feast," said Gompy.

"How thoughtful. That will be lovely," smiled Aunt Em. "Now all of you get to bed and have a good night's sleep, and I'll see you in the morning. You have your cell phone, Rachel?"

"Yes, Em."

"Good. I tried to get the phone company to turn the service on, but they said you would have to fill out all the papers and stuff. But as long as you have your cell, you can call me if you need anything. Please don't hesitate."

"Em, you are a good and true friend. I don't know what we would do without you."

"I'm just glad I'm here and can do a little something to help. You know— oh I'm just going to say this and get it over with—you know how much we loved Ben and love you and the kids. There's so little anyone can do in these situations, but we want to do what little we can. It's an honor and a privilege for us to help." She hugged Rachel, wiped her eyes and started down the stairs.

"I'll get the turkey for you," said Gompy.

Em called back, "I'll see you tomorrow. Call if you need me!"

"I know this is going to sound a little strange, Mom," began Sam, "but I think, despite everything, we are very lucky."

Rachel reached for her children and held them tightly.

"I don't think that sounds strange at all. I think it's absolutely true." She kissed the tops of their heads. "Now, to bed to bed for all of us!"

And as the wind howled around the aptly named house, they retreated to their rooms with their own thoughts to spend their first night in *Windswept*.

7

It was several hours later when Rachel heard a gentle tapping on her door and a small voice whispered, "Mom?"

"Sam, what's wrong?" asked Rachel as she reached for the bedside lamp.

The door creaked open and Sam's head appeared around the edge.

"I couldn't sleep. The branches of the tree outside my window keep hitting the house. It's creepy. Can I sleep with you?"

"Sure—come on," and Rachel drew back the covers inviting her daughter into the warmth of her bed. "It's weird, huh? Being in this house?"

"Yeah—specially being here without—"

"Without Dad?"

As tears threatened, Sam could only nod her head.

"I know. Sometimes, I feel so lonely I want to scream. But you know, other times, I feel like Dad is so close—that he's right here next to me. I really think he is, Sam. He wanted us to have this house and I think he would be really happy that we are here."

"Does that mean we're going to keep it?"

"No, honey. There are a lot of questions to be answered before we can make that decision. About all we can decide this weekend is whether we *want* to keep it. After that, we have to find out if we *can*."

"Mom, you know what you said before," Sam hesitated, not sure she wanted to voice the thought that had formed in her head, "about feeling Dad near you?"

"Yes."

"I—I don't feel that. I keep hoping I will. I look at his picture all the time. I try to remember things we did together. But I just don't feel him near me."

"Sam," crooned Rachel as she put her arms around her, "it's not something you can make happen. Everybody grieves in their own way. Do you remember when Mr. Bridgeman died and Mrs. Bridgeman came back from the funeral and immediately took all of Mr. Bridgeman's clothes to the Salvation Army?" Sam nodded. "Well, a lot of people thought that was strange."

"You didn't do that," observed Sam.

"No, I didn't and that's my point. I like having Dad's things around me. I find all the memories very comforting, but that's the way I am. Remember the year you said you wanted to have eggs and bacon for Christmas morning breakfast instead of coffee cake, and I got so upset?"

"Yeah."

"That's the difference between us. You are actually more like your Dad. I hang on to old memories and traditions. You and Dad always wanted to try new things. Maybe that's why you don't have the same feelings I do. It's not right or wrong. It's just who we are."

"Thanks, Mom," sighed Sam as she snuggled under the covers. "I think I was feeling a little guilty, like I didn't miss him or something, but I know I do."

"Of course you do, sweetheart. And you are entitled to miss him and remember him in your own way. Now let's try to get some sleep. We have a big day tomorrow—or rather, today!" She turned out the light and within moments, both were sound asleep.

• • •

As so often happens after a nor'easter, the following day dawned clear and bright with a brilliant blue, cloudless sky. A strong breeze still shook the trees and the surf was still high enough to splash over the lowest part of the seawall.

Andy awoke with the sunrise. He scrambled out of bed and pulled on the jeans and sweatshirt he had worn the day before. Tiptoeing down the stairs, he grabbed his jacket, slipped out the side door and headed down the hill to the beach.

Standing on the boardwalk looking out over the water, Andy was amazed by how different the beach looked. Sand washed ashore by the previous day's storm covered all but the top step where he stood. The bands of foot-torturing rocks that had driven everyone to wear funny rubber beach shoes during the summer had all but disappeared.

Slipping off his shoes and socks, Andy stepped down onto the still damp sand. He leapt back as his bare feet reacted to the shock of the cold sand. After a moment's thought, he sat down on the top step and put his socks back on, then stepped off again onto the sand. He was sorry he hadn't remembered his sunglasses as he headed down the beach toward the jetty. He gazed out at the ocean and thought how beautiful it looked. He wished he had awakened his mom. They loved to walk the beach together during the summer, searching for the tiny bits of sand washed colored sea glass. A shadow suddenly appeared next to his, and he turned to see Rachel a few feet behind him.

"I thought I might find you here!"

"Sorry—did I worry you?"

"Not really. I know you pretty well by now. When you weren't in the kitchen rummaging about for breakfast, I figured you must be down here. Find anything good?"

"Just started looking." Andy stooped and picked up a piece of frosty white glass with ridges. "Looks like an old soda bottle," he suggested and put the piece in his pocket.

"How'd you sleep?" inquired his mother.

"Good—only it was a little scary. The house whistles when the wind blows."

"I noticed that myself."

"Is Sam okay?"

"Sure—why do you ask?"

"I heard her get up and go into your room. It was late. I figured—"

"What?"

"She gets sad—sadder than any of us really see. I cry a lot, but she doesn't. I think that makes it harder for her. I think she keeps a lot of junk inside."

"How'd you get so smart?"

"I'm not smart—not about most stuff. Just about Sam. I guess it's 'cause we're twins. I read somewhere that twins can sometimes know how the other one is feeling. Sam always knows when I'm sad and I guess I know when she is. The difference is that I don't know what to do to help her feel better."

"Probably not much you can do, tootsie. It takes time."

"Hey, blue!" cried Andy as he reached down for a tiny piece of hard to find blue glass.

"That's a good sign!"

They walked along quietly, heads down, eyes scanning the stretch of small pebbles and shells that edged the shore, occasionally stopping to pick up a piece of the frosted glass—green, brown, white, even the cherished blue from time to time.

As they reached the jetty that defined the entrance to the harbor, Andy clambered up onto the rocks and headed out toward the small signal tower at the jetty's end. Rachel followed. When they reached a large rock near the end that was tilted at a sharp angle, she held out her hand to Andy, as she had done since he was a small boy. He didn't really need the hand; it had just become a habit of many years. Together, mother and son made their way to the end of the jetty and sat looking out over the white-capped sea.

"Are we gonna keep it?"

"Oh boy—you and your sister. I don't know yet. I haven't even thought about it."

"I have."

"And?"

"Well, I am the man of the family now—" He paused to see if she would laugh, but, of course, she didn't. "I think it would be good to, well, to start fresh. If we stay in New Jersey, everything is going to be the same, except Dad won't be there. If we come here, everything will be new. We won't be expecting Dad around every corner. Besides, he wanted us to have this house. It was the last present he gave us. It was as if he knew somehow that he wasn't going to be around. He wanted us to remember him with the house."

"I agree with you. But it's not just about what we want. It's about what we can afford. I'll tell you what—I'll promise you that if there's any way that we can keep this house, we will. That's the best I can do."

"Well, as someone I know and love once told me when I wanted to try out for the basketball team, 'The most anyone can ever ask of you is the best you can do.'"

"Must have been a really smart person," laughed Rachel.

"Yeah," replied Andy, "you are. Now, did you say something about breakfast?"

8

The rest of the day passed in a blur of turkey, stuffing and pumpkin pie.

"I am so full!" groaned Sam as she collapsed on the couch in the living room at *Windswept*.

"I'm freezing," said Rachel. "The fire's gone cold. It must be forty degrees in here."

She crossed to the old pot bellied stove and opened the grate. She stuffed it with newspaper and kindling from a basket nearby. She piled logs on top and struck a match. The newspaper caught and the kindling began to burn. Rachel watched for a few moments to be sure the logs caught and closed the door. Within minutes, they could see the heat rising in waves from the stove and the room soon warmed.

"That was a nice Thanksgiving, don't you think?" asked Rachel.

"Yeah," agreed Andy, "I really liked that chestnut stuffing."

"I wish Mr. Barton hadn't mentioned Daddy. It made Gommy so sad," put in Sam.

"I know, honey, but it was sort of the elephant in the living room."

"Huh?"

"The elephant in the living room—meaning everybody was thinking about it, but nobody wanted to acknowledge it. We can't just ignore the fact that Daddy's gone. It doesn't make it go away."

"Your mother is right," agreed Gompy. "It's by remembering him that we keep him close to us."

Rachel looked over at Sam to see how she would respond to Gompy's comment, but Sam's face gave no hint of how she felt. Instead, she jumped up from the sofa, grabbed Andy's hand and shouted, "Come on, Andy, let's see where those stairs go!"

Hand in hand, the twins ran up the stairs to the second floor. Rachel heard the "stomp, stomp, stomp" as they headed up the narrow staircase that led to the tower which sat atop *Windswept*. Moments later, she heard them coming down and then Sam's head appeared around the banister.

"Mom, it's just like Mrs. Harrington said. There's like a trap door at the top of the stairs and it's padlocked," she called out.

"Well, there's a new wrinkle. Come on down and let's see if we can find the key. There's a teapot in the pantry that's full of old keys. It might be one of those."

The twins hurtled down the stairs and dashed into the kitchen. The pantry was a long, narrow room lined with glass fronted cabinets that would hold all the plates and dishes. There were cupboards for pots and pans below. On the counter that topped the lower cupboards there was a toaster oven, microwave and the all important cookie jar, sadly empty since Mildred Harrington had left. Sam saw no teapot.

"Mom," she called, "where is it?"

"Look in the top cabinet on the far end by the window," called her mother.

Sam moved to the end of the long row of cabinets. There on the middle shelf was a white porcelain teapot. She reached up and took the pot down, setting it on the counter and removing its lid. As promised, the pot was filled with dozens of old keys of every shape and size.

"Oh no," groaned Andy, "it will take hours to try all of these."

"What else have we got to do?" asked Sam as she grabbed the pot and started out of the pantry.

• • •

An hour later, the two discouraged children trudged wearily down the stairs carrying the teapot, now empty of its keys. Their looks of frustration and disappointment made questions unnecessary.

"No luck?" asked Gompy.

"We tried them all," moaned Sam.

"Twice," added Andy.

"Well, then, the key must be somewhere else. Perhaps Mildred Harrington knows. Tomorrow I'll get her number from Aunt Em and we'll give her a call."

The twins' faces lit up and they turned their attention to a board game that occupied them for the rest of the evening.

9

When Sam and Andy arrived in the kitchen for breakfast the next morning, they found they had a guest. A tall man wearing a plaid shirt and blue jeans with rainbow striped suspenders was sitting at the kitchen table. He was sipping coffee from a mug and munching on a piece of toast. Their mother was at the stove supervising a fry pan full of bacon.

"Breakfast is coming," she said. "This is Dan Furman. He's the handyman that Em recommended. He's going to take a look at the house and let us know what he thinks we would need to do."

"Cool," said Andy. "The house sure makes a lot of weird noises."

"Well, these old places do," Dan said as Rachel brought plates of eggs and bacon to the twins. "How's your water pressure?" he asked Rachel.

"The pressure's great. It would practically knock you over."

"That's a good sign. It means the pipes aren't all clogged up with sediment."

"Sediment?" exclaimed Sam, surprised. "We learned about sediment in science class. That's what makes rocks. You can make rocks in your pipes?"

"It is kind of like making rocks in your pipes," replied Dan. "If you cut open an old pipe, you often find what looks like cement lining the pipes. It's really calcium and other minerals that are in the water. When they get hard, it certainly acts like rock."

"Cool!" said Andy.

"Not if it's *your* pipes!" replied Dan. "Well, thanks for the coffee and toast, Mam. Okay if I get going and have a look around?"

"Sure," agreed Rachel.

"I'll need access to your basement."

"The door's right over there. Help yourself."

"Can I go, too?" begged Andy.

"If it's okay with Dan, it's all right with me," said Rachel.

"Fine with me. Come on, buddy. We'll go take a look."

"Cool!"

Sam watched as Andy and Dan opened the door cut into the beadboard wall of the old kitchen. Dan found a light pull hanging from the ceiling. He pulled the chain, and the light revealed an old and somewhat rickety set of stairs leading down into the darkness of the cellar below. After a moment or two, Andy called up from the darkness.

"Hey Mom—Sam—you gotta see this. It's so awesome!"

"I'll bet," laughed Sam. "Probably full of spiders and rats."

"Oh my—I hope not!" cried Rachel.

Just then, Andy came bounding up the stairs and burst into the kitchen.

"There's a dirt floor and this honkin' big water heater and all these pipes and stuff. There are big sets of shelves and they're filled with jars of stuff like peaches and pears and tomato sauce."

"Millie must have been canning things," said Rachel.

"Not cans, Mom," groaned Andy, rolling his eyes, "jars."

"That's what you call it—canning," put in Sam. "You cook the fruit and then put it in the jars and then cook the jars, right Mom?"

"When did you become Martha Stewart? I wouldn't know how to can a peach if my life depended on it, but that sounds right to me."

"I read about it in one of my books."

"You read books about putting fruit in jars?" asked Andy.

"No, silly! It was a historical novel that took place in the eighteen hundreds. People back then canned stuff all the time."

"Why?"

"Because they didn't have freezers or dried foods or canned foods like we buy at the store. If they wanted fruit and vegetables in the winter, they had to can them."

"Why didn't they just buy fresh at the store the way we do?" asked Andy, amazed.

"Because back then, you could only get the fruit and vegetables that local farmers grew in season," said Rachel.

"Not like today when we import stuff from South America and all," instructed Sam.

"Thank you, Professor Sam!"

Sam snorted in disgust at Andy's retort, but secretly she was pleased. Sam was not a girl who worried about people thinking she was "too smart". She liked being told she had a good brain and she knew how to use it.

"Well, cans or jars or whatever—you gotta see the basen geous!" cried Andy.

"Maybe later," laughed Sam. "I'm going to search for that up in the tower."

"Me, too!" shouted Andy, the lure of the basement forgotten. "I'll look upstairs, you look down here."

"Okay!" cried Sam as she headed out to begin the search.

Andy sat for a minute, deep in thought.

"Are you going to look?" she asked.

"Yeah," replied Andy, "but I was just thinking. The basement would be a good place to hide a key, wouldn't it?"

"Just stay out of Dan's way!" cautioned Rachel.

"Deal!" shouted Andy as he started for the stairs.

10

As the quiet of the empty kitchen settled over Rachel, she sighed contentedly and took her own plate of eggs and bacon to the kitchen table. After pouring herself another cup of coffee, she sat at the old wooden table. As she ate her food, she gazed out the window at the small garden that Mildred Harrington had planted in the backyard.

Brown and dried now from the crisp fall weather, you could still see remnants of the color that had once painted the yard. In her mind, Rachel began to plan what she would do with the charming little garden.

"Whoa, girl!" she thought to herself. "You're acting like you've made the decision to keep this place. Don't get your hopes up. You know it's probably not going to happen."

"Penny for those thoughts?" asked a gentle voice behind her. Rachel turned to see her mother-in-law standing by the table in her trademark pink robe and slippers.

"You slept in," commented Rachel.

"Gompy and I were awake pretty late, talking," explained Gommy.

"That's nice," commented Rachel distractedly as her attention was once again claimed by the garden.

"Actually, we were talking about you—well, you and the kids," she added quickly as Rachel turned to look at her. "Rachel, I hope you won't think we're trying to interfere, but—"

"But, you don't think it makes any sense for me to try to keep this house. I know. It doesn't. I just don't want to give up."

"No!" cried Gommy, "that's not it at all. In fact, it's just the opposite. Gompy and I think you *should* keep the house. It's clear how much you all love it—and Ben wanted you to have it. It was the last thing he did for his family. We think it would be a shame for you not to keep it."

"Yeah, well, unless he also left me a lottery ticket with a winning number, I don't think we're going to be able to afford it."

"That's where Gompy and I come in," began Gommy.

Rachel began to protest.

"No please, let me finish."

"Go on."

"You know that Ben was our only child. Everything we have would have come to him when we passed. Now, it will come to the children in trust. We see no reason why you—they—shouldn't have some of it now. We have more than we could possibly need. We have excellent health insurance and investments. Now, obviously, this depends on the results of the contractors' estimates, but if it's not too outrageous, Gompy and I would like to take care of the difference between what you get for the Jersey house and what it will cost to make this one into the dream house that Ben wanted you and the children to have. It may sound selfish, but it would be very comforting for us to help honor Ben's wishes."

Rachel felt tears threatening. She rose and embraced the woman she had come to think of as her own mother in the past few years.

"I don't have words to tell you what this means to me—and to the kids. I admit I had already begun to think about what life would be like here. I kept trying to talk myself out of it. Now I don't have to."

"Does that mean you accept our offer?"

Rachel nodded, and the older woman hugged her tightly.

"Well, for Heaven's sake, here's a cheerful scene," cried Gompy as he entered the kitchen. "A man comes looking for bacon and eggs and finds the place awash in tears. What gives?"

"You do," laughed Rachel. "Mom was just telling me about your beautiful offer of help."

"And?"

"And, you will have shredded wheat for breakfast, old man. And Rachel has agreed to let us help."

"Well, that's fine, fine. Well, not the shredded wheat part!" laughed Gompy.

"Now," went on Gommy, "we wanted to suggest one other thing. I hope this won't sound as if we are complete butt-inskies, but Gompy and I would like to offer to move into your Woodfield house and take care of the kids, while you oversee the renovations here."

"Oh, no," protested Rachel. "I can't let you do that. I'm sure I can find someone to oversee things here."

"Perhaps, but it will slow things down considerably," said Gompy. "If you're here, you can make decisions immediately instead of having to negotiate back and forth. Besides, our offer isn't entirely unselfish. We know that once you move here, we're not going to see the children as much as we do now. We would love to have a stockpile of memories to keep us company when we feel lonely for them."

"You've thought of everything. How kind and generous all of it is. No wonder Ben was such a wonderful man."

"He *was* a nice boy," agreed his mother. "And you were the best thing that ever happened to him, Rachel. You made him very happy. We will always be grateful for that." Tears were threatening again, but a cry of excitement from the basement saved them all from further emotion.

"I found it—I know I found it!" cried Andy as he ran up the basement stairs and into the kitchen. "Hi Gommy! Hi Gomps! 'Scuse me—I gotta find Sam. Hey, Sam!" he yelled, racing from the room.

11

"Come on, Sam—Hurry up!" urged Andy as he dragged his sister up the stairs to the second floor. They hurried down the hall to the narrow twisted set of steps that led upwards to the tower.

"Hold your horses, big shot," gasped Sam, "I'm coming. But if I fall and break my arm, I'm gonna be ticked! Besides, it's probably not even the right key. How'd you find it anyway?"

"I was looking at all the jars, and I came to a whole line of jars that were marked *key limes*."

"That makes sense. Mrs. Harrington always made key lime pies for the bake sale in August."

"Right—I figured, if you were going to hide a *key* in with all those jars, you'd need some way to remember where you put it, so I looked behind all the key lime jars and sure enough, there it was! Well, actually there was a piece of cloth and the key was wrapped up in it."

"What do you know? Maybe we need to change your name to Sherlock. Nice detective work, bro."

"Thanks. Now, maybe you won't laugh so hard when I say I want to be a detective when I grow up!"

"I never laughed!" protested Sam. Andy gave her a skeptical sideways glance. "Maybe I snickered once or twice!" she laughed and ruffled his hair, which he hated.

"Cut it out!"

"Come on, Sherlock. Let's see if that key really does open that trapdoor!"

It was a tight squeeze to get both of them up the tiny twisted staircase, but somehow they managed.

"I can't fit the key in the lock. Move your arm," ordered Andy, exasperated by the tight space. Sam turned nearly on her side and let her long legs hang down the stairs to give Andy more room.

"Okay! The key's in. Ready?"

"Wait a minute. Are you sure we should do this? I mean remember what Mrs. Harrington said—about the noise and the moaning?"

"Aw, I think she was just trying to scare us. I think it was just a story."

"All right, but if Freddie Kruger is up there, remember you'll get it first. Now, hurry up, won't you? I'm about to slide down these stairs."

"You'll stop at the bend, so quit worrying," laughed Andy.

"Very funny! Be careful when you turn the key. It's pretty old and might break easily."

"I know. What do you think I am—a dummy?" retorted Andy and his fingers gently began to twist the key. It moved a tiny fraction and then would turn no further. He applied more pressure, but the key wouldn't budge. He felt a swell of disappointment rise in his chest as he considered that, in fact, this might not be the key.

"What's taking so long?" groaned Sam, who was by now thoroughly uncomfortable in her contorted position.

"It won't turn!"

"Try harder."

"I'm afraid to break it. You try."

"We'll have to trade places," asserted Sam. After several minutes of twisting, turning, unintentional gouging and poking, the twins managed to shift their positions so that Sam was positioned just below the trapdoor. She reached up and gingerly tried turning the key. As had Andy, she found it resistant. She tried again, this time with more force and she let out a shout of triumph as she felt the key begin to turn in the lock. "You must have loosened it up," she said and twisted the key again. She felt, more than heard, a satisfying click as the key fully rotated in the lock. She took off the padlock and pried loose the hasp.

"Okay—now," she gently began to push on the trapdoor. "Easy does it—ugh—"

"What?"

"The trap's been painted shut. Hang on. I'm gonna give it a good shove," replied Sam. She half stood, putting all her weight against the stubborn trapdoor. "Ach—yuck, ach-oo!" She sneezed loudly as the door gave, and she was showered with dust and dead bugs. "This door weighs a ton!" grunted Sam as she pushed harder on it. Suddenly, the weight she had been struggling against evaporated and the door flew open. Sam nearly lost her balance, but Andy, in his enthusiasm, had come up close behind Sam and he kept her from tumbling down the stairs.

"Hurry up! Go up! Go up!" cried Andy.

"Wait—it's pitch dark up there. We need a flashlight."

"But there are windows on all sides. How can it be dark?"

"I don't know!" cried an exasperated Sam. "Maybe they've been boarded up or something. Go get a flashlight. Aunt Em left one in each of our rooms. Mine's on the bedside table."

"Okay. But you gotta wait for me."

"Listen, genius, I'm not going up there by myself. There are probably rats up there. I'll wait. Now go!"

Andy scrambled backwards like a crab down the stairs and returned a moment later with a flashlight. He passed it to his sister who aimed the beam into the opening. Suddenly Sam let out a yelp. She let the trap door slam shut and pushing Andy she yelled, "Andy get down—hurry. Get down the stairs."

"What the—Sam have you gone nuts?"

"Move!" ordered Sam.

Finally at the bottom of the stairs, Sam, gasping for breath, whispered, "Andy—there is someone or something in there. It was looking right at me out of the darkness."

"Hey, is everything all right up there?" called Rachel from the bottom of the stairs.

"Mom, there's something in the tower—I don't know what it is or what to do about it."

"Don't do anything. Stay away from the tower until I see what to do," Rachel cautioned anxiously.

"Can I help, Mam?" asked Dan.

"Oh no—I couldn't ask you—"

"I doubt it's anything—but I'm happy to take a look."

"Well that would be awfully nice of you. I'm afraid the twins won't be satisfied until they see what's in that tower."

"Right then," Dan started up the stairs.

"Dan is coming up to take a look," called Rachel.

"Well now, let's see what we've got here," said Dan a minute later as he climbed the narrow stairs to the tower. "Let me see your flashlight, Sam."

Sam, who with Andy had followed Dan up the stairs, handed her flashlight to Dan who carefully pushed open the trap door.

"It's really dark, isn't it?" asked Sam.

"Yeah, there are boards over all the windows. All right, I'm going in," said Dan.

"We're coming, too," insisted Andy.

"Okay, but stay behind me—just in case."

Sam and Andy clambered up the stairs and into the darkness of the tower.

12

"Gee whiz," complained Andy, "it was just a squirrel."

"I'm sorry your dream of being the first kid on the block with a zombie in the attic has been foiled," laughed Rachel, "and I can't say I'm happy to have squirrels in the house."

"That must be why Mrs. Harrington's father locked the tower," suggested Sam.

"Smart man," said Dan. "Squirrels are persistent little fellas. They can do a lot of damage to an old wooden house like this. They've chewed a hole right through the wall to get in, but I'll get some lumber this afternoon and patch it up."

"Is it safe for the children at the moment? I know Andy is about ready to jump out of his skin if he doesn't get to see what else is up there."

"They should be fine. The squirrels won't come in if there are humans present. Unless of course," he turned to Andy with an evil gleam in his eye, "they're RABID!"

"Ha, ha, very funny!"

Rachel chuckled. "Well then, go on you two and explore, but if you see any squirrel droppings or, Heaven forbid, a squirrel, don't touch it and come right back down, do you hear?"

"Yes, Mom, we will," answered Sam.

"In fact," she rummaged in the cupboard under the sink bringing out two pairs of rubber gloves, "take these." She handed the gloves to Sam.

• • •

"Well, Mam, your plumbing seems to be in pretty good shape. I think there's been some work done on it in the recent past. Your water heater is only about five years old and it's one of the best—real efficient. It's propane, like your stove. There are a couple of sections of pipe that feed the kitchen sink and your washing machine that need to be replaced. You ought to replace them with copper pipe. It's the most expensive, but it's the best. Other than that, you might want to think about replacing the toilets. You've only got three, and they're old. They use a lot of water. The new ones are designed to use a lot less. I don't know about your septic, but things look okay from the inside."

"Yes, Em Michaels told me that Millie had a new system put in four years ago," Rachel said. "My big concern is heat. I mean, the wood stove is fine for a weekend, but if we decide to live here—"

"You're thinking of living here, Mam?" he asked in a surprised voice.

"Yes. Why?"

"Well, Mam, it's not my business of course, but this house, it wasn't built for that. I'm sure you've noticed there's no insulation. And you'd have to put in a mighty big furnace to heat a place as drafty as this."

"Yes, I know. But I was thinking, why couldn't we insulate and then put up interior walls?"

"I guess you could, Mam. You'd lose some space, but these rooms are generously sized. Of course you'd lose some of the charm of the old Cape Cod house, but I guess you could make it up in other ways."

"Yes, by staying warm!" laughed Rachel. "Do you by any chance know a general contractor you'd recommend?"

"Well, since you're asking, I've done some general contracting here on the Island."

"Really? But you were listed in the phone book as a general handy man."

"Yes, Mam. I had some trouble a few years ago. I'll be honest with you. I was drinking pretty heavily, and I made some mistakes. I reckon if you ask around about me, they'll tell you I used to be one of the best in the business, until I started drinking. But I've stopped now. I've been sober for two years."

"That's admirable. It must have been very hard for you. What made you stop?" asked Rachel.

"My little girl, Mam. Hannah. She's nine. Her mother died when she was three. That's when I started drinking. One night, I got drunk and fell asleep with a lit cigarette in my hand. Set the house ablaze. I couldn't get to her on the second floor. If it hadn't been for the firemen, well—I was so horrified by what I'd done, I just stopped. It was as if someone just threw cold water on me."

"I'm so sorry. What a tragedy."

There was an uncomfortable pause.

"So, would you be willing to consider me for the general contractor job, Mam?"

"Well—" Rachel hesitated.

"I haven't made much money lately. I could use the work. My little girl— she needs things. You wouldn't have to pay me till it was all done. That way, if I mess it up, you don't have to pay me at all. I'll sign a contract to that effect."

"That won't be necessary, Dan. But truthfully, I'm still not a hundred percent sure that we're going to keep the house."

"Oh, you're going to keep it. I can tell."

"Really," laughed Rachel, "what makes you say that?"

"You love this house. I can tell by the way you touch things; the way you stroke this old table with your fingers, like it was silk or fur, I can tell you love this house."

"I do. You're right."

"Besides, why would you have bought it if you didn't love it?"

"Well, actually, I didn't buy it. Not exactly, anyway. My husband bought it for us."

"Will he be joining you here, then?"

Rachel felt the tears start and turned away to look out the window over the sink that had a lovely view of the water. She took a deep breath and turned back to Dan.

"No, he won't. My husband was in the North Tower of the World Trade Center on September 11th. He's—" she stopped, afraid to say the words which she had avoided for months, "he's dead."

"I'm very sorry, Mam. I know how hard it is."

"Yes, you do."

After a moment, Dan said, "What do you think? I mean about my proposition."

Rachel thought for a minute. She could hear the arguments raging in her head. Words like "unreliable," "drunkard," "foolhardy" echoed loudly. But another voice said, "This man needs this job. You can do something good for someone." But the argument that decided her was the voice that said, "Ben would have hired him." She turned to Dan.

"All right. We'll try it. But I don't think it's fair to make you wait until the end for your money. Shouldn't we draw up a schedule for when things will be finished and set a payment plan? I'm sure that's the way it's done."

"Thank you, Mam. That's more than fair."

"I think if we're going to renovate this old house together, you'd better call me Rachel. 'Mam' makes me feel so old."

"Yes, Ma—Rachel," said Dan, smiling.

"Will you make a survey of the whole house then and give me a list of what you think we need to do to make it livable on a year round basis? I'll tell you right now, I'm not an air conditioning person, but I do like to be warm in the winter."

"I'll keep that in mind. When would you want to start?"

"As soon as possible, I suppose. It doesn't seem as if we would need to open up the house for anything, so we should be able to work through the winter. I'd like the children to be able to start school here in September."

"Really?" squealed Andy from the doorway to the kitchen.

"Mom, does that mean we're staying?" asked Sam.

"Assuming Dan doesn't give me an estimate bigger than the national debt, I guess it does."

The twins began to hoot and sing and dance around like whirl-i-gigs in a nor'easter.

"We're moving to the Vineyard! We're moving to the Vineyard!" they sang.

"And that means we'll have all the time in the world to find the pirate's treasure!" crowed Andy.

13

"Oh Heaven help me!" cried Rachel laughing. "What is this about pirate treasure?"

Suddenly, both twins were shouting at once.

"We got into the tower. We found—"

"This cool old leather box with all this stuff in it and—"

"Part of it was an old diary from like the eighteen hundreds—"

"Hold on—hold on!" laughed Rachel. "I can't understand a word you're saying. Breathe."

The twins stopped talking and took a breath.

"We—" they began together.

"Sam, you start," commanded Rachel.

"Okay," Sam drew a deep breath. "We got into the tower. At first we didn't think there was anything there. It was so dark and all. But then we found this old wooden chest. It has the initials A.P. on it and when we opened it, it smelled funny—like moth balls."

"It must be a cedar chest," suggested Rachel.

"Whatever—inside the chest was a ratty old quilt, but when we looked underneath it, we found an old leather box. It had A.P. stamped on it, too!"

"Andy, your turn," prompted Rachel as Andy looked like he would burst if he didn't get to tell part of the story.

"So, we opened the box. We knew it was really old because when we went to untie the ribbon around it, it just fell apart. As we lifted off the top, a piece of it cracked off. There was all sorts of junk inside the box. There were some letters—we couldn't read them because the writing is really funny and it's pretty faded. Then there was a little wooden box. Under all that, we found this leather book. At first we thought it might be a Bible or a prayer book or something."

"But it isn't. It's a diary," continued Sam, "and underneath the diary was a map all folded up. It's made on really old paper. We haven't figured out what it's a map of yet, but—"

"But there's words on it and we could make out the words 'pirate treasure' except Mrs. Riefler would have given this person a 'D' in spelling 'cause they spelled pirate 'p-i-r-e-t' and treasure 't-r-e-s-h-o-r.'"

"And she would give you a 'D' in punctuation—you aren't using any! Slow Down!"

"Anyway," continued Sam, "we think it's a map showing where some treasure is buried, but we don't know where or anything. We're hoping we can read the diary and maybe that will tell us."

"Well, it all sounds very exciting, but let's take things one step at a time," cautioned Rachel. "First of all, you don't even know if these things are genuinely old."

"But Mom," protested Sam, "the stuff is so fragile—it has to be really old!"

"I'm not saying it isn't, but it doesn't take long for paper to turn brittle and yellow. And in a closed up tower, I imagine leather would dry out pretty quickly. I think your first stop ought to be the Historical Society. They can probably tell you if it's genuine."

"Yeah, and then they'll say they have to keep it because it's valuable," predicted Andy.

"Maybe we could just take one of the letters," suggested Sam. "That way, if they want to keep it, we'll still have enough information to find the treasure."

"Guys, the Historical Society is not a bunch of artifact thieves. I'm sure they won't try to keep what you've found. On the other hand, they might very well be able to help you decipher the writing. Also, I know that there are some precautions you should take in handling old artifacts, like wearing gloves. They can probably show you how to do it. You don't want to ruin what you've found."

"Why would they help us if we aren't going to let them have the stuff?" asked Andy.

"Well, in the first place, they are historians. They will probably be interested simply because that's what they love. Secondly, you might want to consider donating the artifacts—" Andy began to protest. "After, you have found your pirate treasure!" finished Rachel.

"Yeah—that sounds like a good compromise," said Sam. "After all, what would we do with the stuff once we find the treasure?"

"And plus, we'd probably get our names and pictures in the paper," replied Andy. "So when can we go to the Historical Society?"

"Well, I would very much doubt there would be anyone there today, but we can call," said Rachel. "One of you see if you can find a phone book. I know I saw one somewhere."

"I think it's by the phone in the upstairs hall," suggested Sam.

"You're right," Rachel agreed. "It's on the little shelf of the telephone table."

"I'll get it!" cried Andy as he bolted from the kitchen.

"That young man has a lot of energy," laughed Dan.

"No kidding," said Sam sarcastically.

Moments later, Andy burst through the swinging door clutching the open phone book in his hands, frantically searching.

"Hisslop, Histel, Hittenberg—no Historical Society!" he wailed. "They have to have a phone, don't they?"

"Try the 'M's," suggested Dan.

"But *historical* starts with an 'H,'" lectured Andy.

"Yep," agreed Dan, "but *Martha's Vineyard* Historical Society starts with an 'M.'"

"Oh, yeah, right," replied a slightly embarrassed Andy as he paged through the book. "Martha's Vineyard Hardware, Martha's Vineyard HISTORICAL SOCIETY!" he shouted triumphantly. He ran to the wall phone and picked up the receiver. A puzzled look spread across his face and he jiggled the receiver several times. "Not hooked up," laughed Andy sheepishly.

"Here," said Rachel, handing him her cell phone.

Andy punched in the number he had found. "It's ringing!" he shouted.

"Brilliant, Einstein. You managed to dial the phone. Alert the media!" said Sam laughing.

"Hello? Hello, is this the Historical Society? Cool!" He looked at his sister with a superior stare. "It's the Historical Society, Einstein!" Sam rolled her eyes as Andy rushed on. "My sister and I found some old stuff in the tower of our house with a treasure map and an old wooden box that maybe has a secret compartment or something and a bunch of letters and a diary and we want to know if it's really old so can we bring it over and show it to someone only we don't want to give it to you well not right away anyhow until we find the treasure—"Andy stopped to gulp some air. "Huh?" Andy listened for several moments. "Oh. Okay. Sure, I understand. But when would that be? . . . Thursday?" Andy wailed, "But we're going home on Sunday!" He held the phone against his chest and spoke to his mother. "He says the man who can tell us what we've got is only there on Thursdays. Now what do we do? Oh, I knew this was a mistake."

"Relax," said Rachel. "I'll take the things over on Thursday, and when I come home at Christmas, I'll bring it with me. You won't have time to do anything about it until then anyway, what with school and basketball and everything."

"Mom!" cried Sam. "Aren't you coming home with us? What do you mean Christmas?"

"We'll talk about it in a minute. Andy, give me the phone," demanded Rachel. He did. "Hi, this is the mother of the chatterbox who was just trying to communicate with you," laughed Rachel. "Who am I speaking with? . . . Mr. Stockbridge, I really appreciate your help in this. The children are so excited about their discovery, although I have my doubts about its value. That being said, can you explain to me how we would go about having someone look at the artifacts and give us an opinion as to their authenticity? . . . Mike Farnsworth? . . . Yes, I see. Thursdays from one to four. Do I need an appointment? . . . Oh that would be very kind of you. Let me give you my number in case there is any problem for Mr. Farnsworth." Rachel gave him the number of her cell phone and then said, "Thank you so much for your patience and assistance. . . . You're very sweet. He really is a nice kid—sometimes a bit excitable," said Rachel, glancing sideways at Andy who was jumping up and down and fidgeting. "Well, I don't want to keep you any longer. Thanks again for your help. Goodbye," said Rachel as she hung up the phone.

Andy began shouting, "What'd he say? What'd he say?"

"He said he hoped you would recover," laughed Rachel. Andy looked insulted.

"I'm kidding. He said we, rather I, should bring the things to the Historical Society on Thursday afternoon, and this Mr. Farnsworth will examine them and tell me what if anything we should do next."

"And then you'll call us, right?" prompted Sam.

"Yes, then I'll call you."

"And you won't let them keep the stuff. I mean—it might be valuable and how would we prove it was ours if they tried to keep it?"

"Andy, these gentlemen are respected historians. They run the museum. I don't think they are in the business of stealing artifacts from people."

"Okay—I guess you're right."

"Besides," added Sam, "if they don't keep the stuff, how can they find out if it's real or not? But Mom," Sam continued, "what was that business about Christmas?"

"Remember, I told you before—if we're going to keep this house, we have to do some pretty extensive renovations to make it a year round house. I need to be here, to supervise the work and answer questions, make decisions."

"But what about us? We can't live by ourselves!"

"Of course you can't. Gommy and Gompy are going to move into our house and take care of you. I'll come home as often as I can and you guys will come up on your vacations. The plan is to get the house ready so that when school gets out, you guys will move up here and start school in the fall."

"But Mom," cried Sam, "I don't want to be away from you all that time!"

"Me neither," agreed Andy.

"I know. It's not the ideal situation as far as I'm concerned, either. I don't want to be away from you, but I think it's the only way to get the house fixed by next summer. It won't be easy, but we have to have—"

"A positive attitude!" they all shouted together and fell into each other's arms laughing. Suddenly, Rachel realized that Dan was still in the room.

"Oh, I'm sorry," she apologized. "That's something their dad always said when they complained about anything. It's become a sort of mantra for us to get us through the rough times."

"Well, it seems to work pretty well," said Dan, "and it's a philosophy I would certainly agree with."

"Listen—" Rachel began, looking seriously at her children, "the time will go quickly. You'll be busy and so will I. Soon it'll be June, you'll be promoted to middle school, and the next thing you know, you'll be residents of Martha's Vineyard."

The twins were silent. Rachel could almost see the thoughts whirring around in their heads. Finally, she voiced the concern she thought was uppermost in their minds.

"Look, I think I know what you're thinking. You've lost your dad, and now you think you're losing me. But you're not. I'm just going to be commuting for six months. You'll never get rid of me. I'll go to college with you, and when you get married, I'll live half the year with one of you and half the year with the other."

Sam and Andy looked at each other with horrified expressions and Rachel burst out laughing.

"Very funny, Mom," said Sam. "Okay—we get it. If you can stand it, we can stand it."

"I'd be more concerned as to whether Gommy and Gompy can stand it."

"We can stand it!" cried Gompy from the door. "You folks need to have a more positive attitude!"

Gompy couldn't for the life of him understand why suddenly everyone else in the kitchen, including Dan, was laughing.

14

Sunday morning found them all gathered at the big table in the dining room eating stacks of pancakes and sausages. There wasn't much conversation as each contemplated the months to come.

Rachel wondered how she would deal with the loneliness when the children were gone. She had concentrated so hard on the kids that she hadn't given herself a chance to deal with the hole that Ben's death had left in her world. She hoped she could handle it now. She worried, too, that she didn't know enough about construction and renovations to make intelligent decisions, but she felt that she could trust Dan. Besides, she knew there were plenty of people on the island she could go to for advice. "I'm not a stupid woman," she told herself. "What I don't know, I can learn."

Andy worried mostly about who would help him with his homework and what he would have for lunch. Mom made the best sandwiches. Maybe he could ask her to tell Gommy how to make them right. And did Gompy know anything about math? After all, he was a retired lawyer. How much math does a lawyer need to know? And what would basketball games be like without Mom there to cheer him on and serve the water and orange wedges to the team at halftime?

Sam wondered who would French braid her hair for her. She guessed she could learn to do it herself. And who would drive her soccer team to the away games? Nobody else's mom took them for ice cream or pizza afterwards. And no one else's mom let them play the music they liked on the radio.

Gommy and Gompy wondered if they remembered how to handle young people on a daily basis. Were they strong enough? Would they be too strict? Too lenient? What would they do if the kids didn't like living with them? How would they help them deal with the loneliness they were bound to feel without Rachel?

Sam looked at the others one by one. Each seemed deep in his or her own thoughts. "The elephant's back, Mom," she joked.

Rachel looked up and she, too, surveyed the people around her. She smiled. "Guess we'd better deal with it," she said and took a deep breath. "Okay, I suggest we go around the table and each share our feelings about what we're facing here. Maybe if we talk about it, we can avoid some of the problems that are bound to arise over the next few months."

One by one, they went around the table and voiced the thoughts they had been holding silently. As each spoke, looks of surprise appeared on the others faces. None of them had thought what the upcoming separation might mean to anyone else in the family. As they began to clear the dishes, they had also cleared their hearts and minds, and each member of the family felt ready to deal with what lay ahead.

After the breakfast dishes were washed, dried and put away, they got their coats and went out for a long walk around the Chop before heading back to *Windswept* to pack. As the minutes ticked away, Rachel became quieter and quieter. Finally, as Gompy was loading the car to head for the ferry, Gommy approached her daughter-in-law and put her arms around her.

"I can only imagine what these past months have been like for you, Rachel. And I know that saying goodbye to the children will be very hard for you. I hope you know how much we love them—and you. We can never take your place, but we'll try to be good stand-ins."

"I know, Mom—I'm sure once things get moving on the house, I'll be so busy I won't have time to think about being lonely. It's just that right now, I feel this strange kind of sadness. It's what my mom would have called *bone deep*. I know I'll be okay in a little while. I'm so grateful to you and Dad for all you are doing. After all, you're disrupting your entire lives to help me do this. I won't let you down."

"You couldn't!" reassured Gommy. "Now, Gompy will call Bill Littlefield tomorrow morning and Bill will get the paperwork rolling. It's a blessing that we both use Bill. It eliminates a lot of hassle. He thinks we can have the money in your account by the end of this week or early next week at the latest, so there's no reason that work can't start right away."

"Oh, that is great! I was awake most of last night making notes and sketching ideas. I'll sit down with Dan tomorrow and we'll get started."

"I like Dan. He seems like a steady, knowledgeable, no-nonsense kind of guy. I know he has some, shall we say, history, but I think he's going to do a wonderful job."

"Me, too. But it's nice to hear that you feel that way, too."

"Don't doubt yourself, Rachel. Ben always believed in you, sweetheart, and so do the children. Now, you have to believe in yourself."

"I will!" said Rachel with more confidence than she felt.

Just then the twins burst into the room. Rachel laughed as she thought to herself that they *always* seemed to burst into rooms. "Don't ever try to sneak up on anybody, you two!" she teased.

"Now Mom," began Andy, "you're not going to forget to go to the Historical Society on Thursday and show them what we found, right?"

"Right!"

"And if it is real," continued Sam, "you have to bring the map when you come for Christmas, so we can plan how we're going to find the treasure."

"Right—I've got it!"

"Time to go," said Gompy quietly, hating to be the messenger who had to deliver the bad news. They had all decided that Rachel would not go to the boat with them, but now as the twins buckled themselves into the back seat of Gommy and Gompy's car, she wondered if she should go. There was a terrible pulling sensation in her heart and try as she would to stop them, the tears began to slide down her cheeks.

"Oh Mommy, please don't cry," begged Sam as her own tears began. "I'll never be able to go if you cry."

"Okay, okay, okay!" Rachel said as she wiped fiercely at the tears. "No tears! I love you. Be good and I'll talk to you tonight when you get home. Gommy, Gompy, drive safely!"

"We will. We'll call you tonight." said Gompy as he backed the car out of the driveway onto the road. As they drove off to the ferry, Sam and Andy twisted in their seats to wave goodbye to their mom who stood in the middle of the road, the tears now coming freely and matching those on the faces of her two beloved children. As the car disappeared around the corner, Rachel walked numbly back up the path to the front door. She stood on the porch, not wanting to go back into the now empty house, but the cold damp breeze from the sea chilled her quickly, so she opened the front door and went in.

15

The next few days passed in a whirlwind of meetings with Dan as he presented information that would enable Rachel to make intelligent choices about the renovations. By Thursday, she was relieved to have an excuse to escape the house and she whistled happily as she drove along the beach road on her way to the Historical Society.

Parking was not a problem at this time of year. How different it was from the summer, Rachel thought, when the island population swelled to ten times its winter numbers. Residents always said if you hadn't done your errands by eight-thirty in the morning, forget about it!

She parked her car on the street outside the gray shingled buildings that held the Historical Society library and the wonderful little museum that contained all sorts of artifacts illustrating the history and geography of the island. She paused to admire the giant Fresnel lens that stood prominently in the yard of the Society. Clutching the map and the diary, Rachel entered the museum and approached the elderly lady at the desk.

"May I help you?"

"Yes, thank you. I'm Rachel Bennett. I have an appointment with Mike Farnsworth."

"You'll find him in the library. That's the next building over. Just go out this door and go left."

"Thank you so much," said Rachel, who went out the way she had entered.

The library was a small version of the classic library. Shelves held a variety of books, journals, and other materials related to the history of the Vineyard and several wooden tables provided space for researchers to examine them. Rachel approached an elderly gentleman sitting at a desk.

"Excuse me, I'm Rachel Bennett. Are you Mr. Farnsworth?"

"Goodness, no. Mike's in the back. Mike," called the man, "you're appointment's here. And don't dawdle. She's real pretty!"

"Thank you," laughed Rachel.

A tall man, perhaps thirty years old, came in and approached Rachel with a broad smile. He extended his hand, and she shook it.

"Sorry about Pete—he's forever trying to fix me up."

"That's very generous of him," replied Rachel.

"Yeah, except for the fact that I'm engaged to a wonderful girl and we're going to be married in a month!"

"Oh, that does change things a bit."

"Hogwash!" cried Pete. "It's still not too late to change your mind."

"I don't think your daughter would think much of that suggestion," retorted Mike.

"You're engaged to his daughter?" asked Rachel incredulously.

"More's the pity," laughed Pete.

"Yeah, cause now you're going to have to cook for yourself!" laughed Mike. Turning toward Rachel he said, "Don't worry about Pete, he's only half crazy. Now, what can I do for you Mrs. Bennett?"

"Rachel, please."

"Rachel it is. So how can I help?"

"Well, I hope this won't be a waste of your time, but my children discovered some things in the attic of our house, and they are convinced they have stumbled upon some priceless artifacts that will lead them to a fortune in pirate treasure," Rachel laughed. "Now that I actually say it out loud, it sounds completely preposterous!"

"Well, don't worry about it. Most of my investigations have an element of the preposterous. Let me see what you've got."

Rachel handed him the diary and the map. He took them to one of the tables and sat down. After putting on white cotton gloves, he read several pages in the diary and using a small hand lens that he took from his shirt pocket, he examined the map, turning it over and running his fingers over its surfaces. He carefully examined the cover and the binding of the diary and then went to a shelf and retrieved a large volume. After a few minutes, he apparently found what he was looking for and closed the book.

"Well, obviously I haven't given these things a thorough scientific examination, but from a surface inquiry, I think the kids might have something here."

"You're kidding!" exclaimed Rachel, her eyes wide with surprise.

"It's possible," he cautioned. "It appears that the diary was kept by the daughter of a farmer on Chappaquiddick. She was born in eighteen eleven. We know this because she received the diary for her seventeenth birthday and kept it from eighteen twenty-eight to eighteen thirty. The construction of the diary and the materials used seem appropriate for the period. Of course, there are more sophisticated analysis techniques that we'd need to use to be sure, but I would say the diary is quite possibly genuine. The map, on the other hand, is more problematic. It is drawn on what appears to be old paper. However, there's no date of any kind, although there may be some reference to the map in the diary. If we can establish some timeline for the map, we can try to figure out if the artifact fits the time period. I guess what I'm saying is, it will take a while."

"I understand," said Rachel. "Would there be a charge for the authentication?"

"I will ask a friend of mine in Boston to do the work. Since it's for kids, I'm pretty sure he won't charge a lot, but you could probably count on about two hundred and fifty dollars. We would ask for first refusal on the items, should they prove to be genuine and should your children want to sell or donate them to a museum."

"That certainly seems fair. And my children will be relieved to know that you don't intend to steal their find."

"Excuse me?"

Rachel laughed. "They were so sure that they had a genuine treasure map that they were afraid you would steal it from them and go and find the treasure yourself. Is there any real chance that there is pirate treasure buried on Martha's Vineyard?"

"Actually, yes—well, sort of. There is some evidence that pirates did visit the island. There is a legend that a farmer on Chappaquiddick saw pirates burying treasure, but he could never find it. Tom Le Grange now owns the property nearest to where the incident supposedly happened."

"Wow!" exclaimed Rachel. "The kids will be thrilled with that story—even if the map isn't real. But I'm afraid Mr. Le Grange may find himself fending off a couple of ten year olds."

"I don't think he would mind a bit. I would be happy to introduce them to Tom when they're ready to start their search," laughed Mike. "And who knows, maybe the map is real and they'll be the ones to find the treasure."

"Maybe so. Well, how do we proceed?"

"I'll send the map and the diary to my authenticator in Boston. He's really busy, so it will probably take a while—several months in fact."

"That's incredibly kind of you. I know the kids will be thrilled."

"No problem." He paused briefly before asking, "How long have you lived on the island?"

"Well, actually, we don't live here—not yet anyway—well, not officially. I'm staying here supervising renovations on our house, but the kids are staying with my in-laws in New Jersey."

"With your in-laws?"

"Yes. My husband, Ben, was killed on nine-eleven. He bought the house for me as a fifteenth wedding anniversary gift. The kids and I decided that we should keep it, but the only way we could afford that was to move here, so that's the plan."

"Gosh, I'm sorry. It must have been awful for you."

"It still is. I guess it always will be. But thank goodness I have two wonderful kids."

Rachel paused and then extended her hand. "Well, thanks so much for all your help, Mike. The kids will be very excited, and I'm sure they'll want to go treasure hunting when they get back on the island in June."

"Maybe by then I'll have some answers for them. In the meantime, I'll make a sketch of the map and drop it off, if you'll tell me where you live."

"Sure. The house is called *Windswept*, it's—"

"Millie Harrington's house?"

"Yes, do you know Millie?"

"Sure, she was one of our best volunteers."

"Oh, of course. I forgot that she used to volunteer for the Historical Society."

"That's great that you are in her house. She must be delighted. She loved that old place."

"Indeed she did. So do we. Or at least, we will as soon as we have some heat!"

16

It took Rachel almost half an hour that night to explain to the twins what she had learned from Mike Farnsworth. She was constantly interrupted after each new revelation with shrieks and shouts and suggestions of how they would spend their money.

"Will you two please calm down? There's no money yet and probably won't be. We don't even know if the map is genuine. And you will have to pay the authenticator's fee. It's a good thing you've put your birthday money in the bank all these years! Besides, no one has ever found the treasure, so what makes you think you will?"

"We've got as good a chance as anybody. And we have the map, so maybe our chances are even better," protested Andy.

"Besides," added Sam, "you've got to have—"

"A positive attitude!" they all shouted together.

"All right—we'll have a positive attitude. But as I told you, Mike won't know anything for several months."

"So we should know just about the time we get out of school and move up there, right?" said Sam.

"Right," agreed Rachel. "Now, the other thing you need to do is contact Millie Harrington."

"Why?" asked Andy.

"Because the diary and the map are really hers—"

"But—" Andy interrupted

"I know, I know—she sold us the house furnished. Still, I think it's only right to let her know what you've found and what might happen. I want you to write her tonight and let her know. Don't worry, Andy. I'm sure she will want you to go ahead. Gommy has her address."

"We'll do it, Mom. Don't worry," Sam assured her.

"So Mom—tell us about the house? What's happening? Did they start yet?" asked Andy.

"Good Heavens, no!" laughed Rachel. "Dan and I have been talking. We made a list of all the things I want to do and put them in order of importance. We'll be meeting with contractors for the next few weeks getting estimates. Then we'll have to see what we can afford to do. You guys better get used to the idea that none of this is going to happen quickly," she warned.

"As long as it happens!" replied Sam.

"It will happen—I promise. Now, let me speak with Gommy, would you?"

The rest of the call consisted of Gommy giving blow by blow descriptions of the twins' activities. They all seemed to be settling into the routines of living together, and Gommy was obviously enjoying spending time with her grandchildren.

"Oh Gommy—you're the best. I wish I was there. I hate missing these moments with my kids."

"There will be plenty more. You have your priorities straight, Rachel dear. First and foremost, you need a home for the twins to come to. Now, tell me, how are things working out with Dan?"

"Wonderfully, so far. He's very knowledgeable and I'm sure he will be a great help with the sub-contractors. He knows all the right questions to ask. He'll be invaluable in helping me to understand the bids and make smart choices. He does keep warning me that everything is going to be much more expensive than it would be in New Jersey, so I'm not sure how much of our dream house we're actually going to get, but I suppose as long as it's structurally sound, warm in the winter and has indoor plumbing, the rest can wait!"

"That sounds like a very practical approach. And with your creativity, you will make it beautiful, just as you have this house," Gommy assured her.

"Thanks, Gommy. I appreciate all the support you and Dad are giving me and the kids. We couldn't do any of this without you."

"Well, you probably could—but I'm glad you're not. Believe me, we're getting as much if not more out of this as we're putting in. Now, let me put the children back on for a minute. They want to say goodnight."

As they reluctantly ended the call, mother and children exchanged good night wishes and long distance kisses.

As Rachel sat with a cup of tea in the drafty old kitchen, she allowed herself to remember some of the wonderful times she and Ben had shared with the twins.

"I'm so proud of them, Ben," she whispered. "They've come through like champions. They're so much like you. I'll never really lose you as long as I have them."

She turned out the lights and took her tea up the narrow twisting stairs to her bedroom where she settled in with a book. She had read only a page before she was dreaming of paint and wallpaper.

17

The following Wednesday, the phone rang just as Rachel was getting ready for bed.

"Hello?" she answered.

"Rachel, dear, it's Gommy," said the voice on the other end. Rachel went cold.

"What's wrong? Is someone hurt?"

"No, dear, no. I'm sorry to have frightened you. It's just—well, I wanted to wait until Sam had gone to bed so we could talk freely."

"Why?" asked Rachel a bit frantically.

"I'm just a bit concerned. Everything was going so beautifully. I guess it was unrealistic to expect that we would have completely smooth sailing."

"Gommy, what's going on?"

"Sam has suddenly gotten very quiet, almost withdrawn. I asked Andy if he knew what the trouble was, but he claims not to. He is very concerned about her, too, although he doesn't say much. I can tell, though, by the way he has stopped teasing her. Rachel, I know you have a lot on your plate right now, but I think you need to come down here. I know we're coming up at Christmas, but I don't think you should wait that long. Sam needs you."

"Of course I'll come, Gommy. I'll come Friday. There won't be any house stuff to deal with over the weekend. And even if there is, Dan can handle it. I'll get on the first boat I can."

"Thank you, dear," responded Gommy gratefully. "It's all well and good to be the doting grandparent, but when it comes right down to it, there's no substitute for your mother. Drive carefully, dear, and we'll see you Friday."

After she hung up, Rachel began to speculate on what might be upsetting Sam. She had at first assumed that it was just a delayed reaction to Ben's death, and she was still leaning toward that conclusion, but other ideas also presented themselves. Sam was almost eleven. Rachel knew that many of her friends had already reached puberty and wondered if that could be it. She remembered how much she had needed her mother at that time in her life. Then she wondered if there was a boy involved. Sam was so open to people, Rachel had always thought it would be difficult when she began to date. The very word 'date' filled her with dread. Sam was much too young to be thinking about that sort of thing, but Rachel knew that social relationships were beginning earlier and earlier. The one thing she felt fairly certain of was that the problem was not related to school work. Sam was a first rate student and really loved learning and school. "Well," she thought as she tried to get comfortable and fall asleep, "I guess I'll find out Friday."

. . .

"Mom!" shouted Andy on Friday afternoon as he barreled through the kitchen door and saw his mother. Rachel was sitting at the table with Gommy having a cup of tea. "We didn't know you were coming. How long are you staying?"

"Mom?" said Sam incredulously. She ran to her mother and threw her arms around her, hugging her so tightly that Rachel was afraid she might stop breathing. Sam abruptly pulled away and looked seriously at Rachel.

"Mom—is everything okay? You're not sick or anything are you? The house didn't burn down, did it?"

Rachel would have laughed if the look in Sam's eyes hadn't been so serious.

"No, sweetheart. I'm fine, the house is fine, everything is fine. I just missed you guys and decided that a weekend down south would be a good idea. Now let me look at the two of you." She held them at arms length. "I think you've both grown a foot!"

"Mom, it's only been two weeks since we saw you," laughed Andy.

"It seems like three months," responded Sam quietly.

"It does to me, too, Sam," replied Rachel.

"How long are you gonna stay?" asked Andy.

"Just for the weekend. I have a reservation on the eight-thirty boat on Sunday. So we better not waste a minute. How about dinner out?"

"Oh darn—I can't!" wailed Andy. "I have a basketball game. Can you come?"

"Sure. Sam and I will have an early dinner and then we'll come to the game. How does that sound?" she asked, looking at Sam.

"Sounds good to me," said Andy, "if we can go for ice cream after the game."

"Absolutely! How about it Sam? Sound okay to you?"

"Sure, Mom."

"But what about Gommy and Gompy?" asked Andy.

Gommy laughed. "Your grandfather and I have made plans for the evening. We're going dancing!"

"Good for you, Gommy. You two deserve a night out on the town," cheered Rachel.

"Now, now—don't make it sound like we've been put upon being with the twins. They are a joy to be with. I never have to ask for help in the kitchen or around the house, they just volunteer. And they both keep their rooms nice and neat," she finished.

"Okay, who are you and what have you done with the real Andy?" laughed Rachel, tousling Andy's hair.

"Hey, come on, Mom, quit it! You told us to be good and try to help Gommy. I was just doing what you asked," protested Andy.

"Another first!" teased Rachel. "All right, so we have a plan. Gommy and Gompy will trip the light fantastic, Sam and I will have an early dinner, and then watch Andy mop up the court with—who are you playing?"

"Rocky Glen."

"With Rocky Glen—and then the three of us will gorge ourselves on hot fudge sundaes at Brimmer's. Any objections?"

This question was answered with a chorus of 'no's—except for Sam who said nothing.

"And tomorrow, we'll have a nice family dinner," said Gommy. "I have a beautiful roast in the fridge."

"Sounds great, Gommy," said Rachel. "Now, I guess you had better have something to eat, Andy. Sam, why don't you change and figure out where we want to eat. We can drop Andy off at school on our way."

"There's a new place—Miller's—on Main Street. Al Franks said they have great burgers. Why don't you go there?" suggested Andy.

"How does that sound, Sam?" asked Rachel.

"Whatever you want is fine, Mom," said Sam quietly, and Rachel felt a little shiver of anxiety.

18

A n hour later, seated in a booth at the restaurant with their cheeseburgers and fries in front of them, Rachel asked the question she had wanted to ask Sam since she had arrived.

"Honey, you seem awfully quiet. Is something troubling you that I can help with?"

"I don't know, Mom. I don't think anybody can help," replied Sam as tears welled in her eyes.

"What is it, baby? Tell me."

"Oh, it's stupid really," said Sam, angrily wiping the tears away that had run down her cheeks. "They're having a banquet to celebrate the end of the soccer season."

Rachel looked confused and Sam continued. "It's a—" her voice caught and more tears escaped. "It's a father-daughter dinner!" she blurted out and could not hold back a great gasping sob as the tears came full force. She held her napkin in front of her face until it was soaked through.

"Oh, baby, I'm sorry," said Rachel softly, feeling as if her heart would break. She rooted through her purse for a small packet of tissues and shoved them into Sam's hand. "I think it was pretty thoughtless of the coaches. They certainly know that you just lost your dad. "

"I don't think they meant to upset me. Let's face it, Mom, people forget really quickly. Life goes on for them. It's just for us that life seems to have stopped."

"How did you get so smart, so fast?" Rachel asked, astonished at her child's understanding.

"I had smart parents!" laughed Sam. "I'm sorry I got so upset. It's just a stupid dinner. Who wants to go anyway?"

"You do," replied Rachel, desperate to think of something she could say that would help. Suddenly, she had an idea. "What if you went with Gompy?"

"Gompy?" asked Sam incredulously.

"Why not?"

"I guess it would almost be like going with Daddy, since Gompy is his father."

"And I know Gompy would be pleased to be asked."

"I should have known you'd be able to help," said Sam quietly. "How do you always show up when I need you the most?"

"Well, in this case, you better thank Gommy. She called me. She was worried about you."

"I guess I better stop feeling sorry for myself. I've got two mothers!" she laughed. After a moment she asked shyly, "Can I get a new dress?"

"Excuse me? A dress?" cried Rachel in stunned surprise. "Samantha Bennett has actually asked for a dress?"

"Mom!" protested Sam.

"Well, I'm sorry, honey, but the last time I tried to get you into a dress for your cousin Edith's wedding you staged a revolution that would have made the Minute Men proud!"

"Well, that was almost two years ago. I'm entitled to change, aren't I?"

Rachel laughed, "As long as you don't do it too fast!"

"So what about the dress?"

"We'll go shopping tomorrow!" Sam's face lit up with a smile. "Now, we'd better eat these burgers or we'll be late for the game."

• • •

"Did you see that lay up that Mark made? He is so good!" exclaimed Andy a few hours later in between mouthfuls of Rocky Road, hot fudge, nuts, coconut, and whipped cream.

"Andy, please! Not with your mouth full. It's gross!" chastised Sam as she delicately spooned some of her coffee ice cream with hot butterscotch and pecans. Andy stuck out his tongue.

"Mom!" cried Sam, "make him stop!"

"Andrew—that will be enough," admonished Rachel. "Just because you made the game winning rebound doesn't mean you are allowed to gross out your mother and sister in a public place!"

Sam and Andy both laughed. "Sorry, Mom," Andy apologized, still laughing. "So, do you think you can come back for the playoffs?"

"I don't know. We'll have to see, sweetie. It will all depend on the house. I'll try."

"Okay. Hey, tomorrow can we go to the park? They're having a battle of the bands with all these bands from the high school. And there's a skateboarding festival, too."

"I think we can work that into the schedule," said Rachel. "Sam and I have a little shopping to do in the morning, but then I don't see why we can't go to the park afterwards."

"What are you shopping for?"

"A dress."

"Not one word, Andrew Jason Bennett or you will be wearing that disgusting concoction instead of eating it!" threatened Sam.

"I didn't say anything!" protested Andy.

"Yeah—but you thought it!"

"Well, your closet's not exactly full of dresses. What's the special occasion?"

"The soccer banquet," replied Sam.

"You're going? But I thought—" he stopped

"You thought what?" snarled Sam.

"Hey, chill. I thought it was a father-daughter dinner and well—" he stopped.

"Sam is going to ask Gompy to take her."

Andy's face lit up. "Wow, that's a great idea!"

"You really think so?" asked Sam, surprised.

"Sure. Saved by the bell!"

"What do you mean?" asked Sam

"I was going to offer to take you."

"You were?" gasped Sam.

"Well, somebody has to take care of you, knucklehead."

"Oh, Andy! That's the dearest thing I've ever heard," said Rachel

"Oh for gosh sakes, Mom," said Andy blushing, "I didn't want her to have to go alone, or worse, not to go at all. Especially since I bet she's going to get the MVP award."

"I doubt that," protested Sam.

"Betcha a dollar!"

"Deal!"

• • •

"Mom, when are we going to see you again?" asked Sam as her mother put her suitcase into the car on Sunday afternoon.

"Three weeks. Gompy made the ferry reservation for the twenty-third—the last day of school. It'll be Christmas on the Vineyard."

"What? I thought you were coming here!" cried Sam

"I was, but Gommy and Gompy thought you guys would enjoy having Christmas on the Vineyard. There are all sorts of church bazaars and special concerts. It should be fun."

"That is so cool," said Andy.

"But three weeks seems so long," said Sam, her voice trembling.

"It will pass quickly," said Rachel. "You'll be so busy shopping for my Christmas present, you won't know where the time has gone!" she laughed and so did Sam.

"Drive carefully, Mom," cautioned Andy, "and be sure to let us know if that guy from the Historical Society finds out anything about our map."

"I promise. Be good for Gommy and Gompy, and I'll call you tomorrow." Rachel hugged the children and her in-laws, before buckling herself in and driving off down the street. In the rear view mirror, she saw the kids waving. She thought she saw Andy wipe away tears, but she couldn't be sure.

19

"So what do you think, Dan?" asked Rachel ten days later as they sat drinking coffee at the kitchen table on a cloudy Monday morning.

"Well, Lansfield is the low bid, but the Middleton bid includes a lot of detail work that Lansfield doesn't. It's work you'd need or want to have done and it will cost a lot more to do it after the fact. The other bids are way out of line and your price range. My guess is they're too busy to do the job, but they don't want to just turn it down."

"So, you think we should go with Middleton?"

"They do good work. I don't think you would have any complaints. They stay on budget and they get the work done on time. I don't know Lansfield as well. And like I said, in the end, you're going to want the detail work. It's more a question of whether you can afford the extra. It is about sixty-five hundred more than you said you wanted to spend."

"Luckily, Ben always told me to low ball everything," Rachel smiled. "I think I can handle the extra, and it would be better to have it done right the first time." Rachel took a deep breath. "Okay, let's do it. Call Middleton, tell them they have the job and find out when they can start. I really want this done by the end of June when the kids get here."

"I don't think that should be a problem," assured Dan. "When can they start?"

"Well, I guess I'd like them to hold off until the kids go home after Christmas, so January second?"

"I think that will probably suit them, too."

"Good. Now I need a favor."

"Sure. What?"

"Can you give me a hand getting the Christmas tree into the house and into the stand? I always did it with Ben, but—" Rachel's voice trailed off.

"No problem. Where's the tree?"

"In a bucket of water in the garage. I've got the stand all ready in the living room."

"Well, let's do it."

A half hour later, the two were laughing so hard, the tears were streaming down their cheeks. The tree was nearly seven feet tall and they were struggling to make the turn into the side door which opened into the living room.

"Next time we should go around to the front door. It's a straight shot from there," suggested Dan.

"Now you think of it," laughed Rachel. "Lead on!"

Finally, the tree was wrestled into submission and stood proud and tall in the living room.

"It's a real nice tree," said Dan.

"It is nice," agreed Rachel. "Have you bought yours yet? I can recommend the place I bought mine."

"Oh, thanks—" Dan hesitated, "but we won't be having a tree."

"What?" cried Rachel. "No Christmas tree for Hannah? And speaking of Hannah, when do I get to meet her?"

"Oh, I'll bring her with me sometimes to the job—uh, if that's all right with you. She knows how to stay out of the way."

"But what about Christmas and a tree?" asked Rachel.

"Well, the truth is, we're sort of between houses at the moment."

"What do you mean?"

"We were renting a little place out on County Road, but the owners sold it. The new ones didn't want to rent, so we had to get out. We haven't been able to find anything I could afford."

"But where have you been staying?" asked Rachel.

"In my van," said Dan quietly, his face turning crimson.

"Oh, Dan," said Rachel softly, gently touching his arm, "why didn't you tell me?"

"Embarrassed, I guess."

"Dan, you can't live in your van. There must be a solution," Rachel paused, thinking. Then she cried, "Oh my gosh, how stupid am I? The garage!"

"The garage?"

"Yes. The back of the garage is a little apartment. It's full of stuff at the moment—lawn furniture, beach umbrellas and what have you, but if we cleaned it out, it would be livable. There's a bedroom and a little alcove that could be Hannah's bedroom and a nice living room with a kitchen area at one end, and a bathroom. It has heat and hot water. It wouldn't be luxurious, but it would be comfortable, I think. We can paint and put up new curtains and—"

"Hold on, hold on," interrupted Dan. "I can't let you do this, Mrs.—Rachel. It wouldn't look right. What would people say?"

"Oh piffle. I think they would say that a nice man and his daughter have a decent place to live. Besides, I don't care what people say. Now, let's go out and see what needs to be done to make this apartment livable by the time Hannah gets out of school!"

And with that began a morning of dragging and lifting. By lunch time there was a large pile of old porch furniture, window screens from days past, assorted beach toys, an old push lawn mower and several large garbage cans full of smaller debris sitting in the driveway ready to be carted to the dump.

"After lunch, we'll clean, and then we can see about some furniture," said Rachel as she wiped the sweat from her forehead, leaving a large dirt smudge in its place. "It really needs to be painted," she said as she surveyed the now empty apartment. "Perhaps I was over confident when I said we could have it ready by tonight, but you and Hannah can stay in the main house with me until we get it ready."

"Oh no—absolutely not," said Dan.

"Do you want to be my general contractor?" asked Rachel.

"Yes, Mam, but—"

"Then, don't call me 'Mam' and don't argue with me about this. Your daughter is not going to spend one more night in that van. And neither are you.

If we work hard, I imagine we can get you moved in by Thursday night. Now, let's have some lunch and then you can go to Vineyard Haven and buy some paint and supplies. Meanwhile, I'll see what I can do about furniture, curtains, and kitchen supplies. We'd better plug in that fridge and make sure it works, too."

"No offense, but do you always boss people around like this?" asked Dan.

"Only when they are being pigheaded and stubborn."

20

It was a very tired Dan that picked Hannah up after school that afternoon. "Hi Daddy!" cried Hannah as he swung her up from the ground and kissed her on both cheeks. "You seem awful happy."

"I am, little one! I am. I think maybe our luck has changed."

"You found a house for us to rent?"

"Well, sort of. Mrs. Bennett said we can stay in the apartment out back of her garage. She spent the whole morning with me fixing it up, and by Thursday it will be about the nicest place we've ever lived. We're going to stay in the big house with her until it's ready."

"She sure seems nice. When do I get to meet her?"

"How about right now?" asked Dan as he turned onto East Chop Drive and headed up the hill to *Windswept*.

As they pulled into the driveway, Rachel came out onto the side porch. She wiped her hands on the old shirt she had been wearing while she painted and crossed the yard to the little girl and her father.

"Hannah, I'm Rachel," she said extending her hand.

"How do you do?" replied Hannah and made the little curtsy her father had taught her.

"I'm just fine, thank you, Hannah. And I'm so glad you're going to be staying here. You know, I have two children—Sam and Andy. They're twins. They're living in New Jersey until the house is renovated and I miss them so much. It will be wonderful to have a child living here."

"It's very kind of you to let us stay here," replied Hannah. "How old are the boys?"

Rachel laughed. "Oh, I'm sorry. I should have explained. Sam is a girl. They're almost eleven. They're in fifth grade."

"I'm nine going on ten. I'm in fourth grade. How can a girl be named Sam?"

"Hannah, mind your manners," cautioned Dan.

"No, no—it's a perfectly good question. Her real name is Samantha, but we call her Sam for short. She's a bit of a tomboy, so the name suits her! Now, come along and let me show you where you're going to sleep tonight."

An hour later, Rachel and Hannah were chatting like old friends while Dan looked on no longer even trying to get a word in.

"And then, just as we were getting ready to go home, we heard this awful scream. The frog had gotten into Mrs. Pomfret's purse, and when she opened it, it jumped out at her. It was so funny!" laughed Hannah. "This year Mrs. Pomfret refused to have the frogs. She did hermit crabs instead. She said at least they wouldn't be able to get into her purse!"

"It sounds like quite a lesson!" laughed Rachel. "What are your favorite subjects besides science?"

"I really like social studies—you know, history and all."

"Well, then you will be interested in what Sam and Andy found in the house. It was an old diary and a map. I took them over to the Historical Society so they could find out if they are real. If they are, I'll bet Sam and Andy would love to have your help when they go looking for the pirate treasure."

"Pirate treasure?" exclaimed Hannah. "Really?"

"Yes! Of course, we aren't sure the map is genuine, but you never know!"

"Well, I think it's real!" asserted Hannah.

"Young lady, do you have homework?" asked Dan.

"Yes, Daddy. Two pages of spelling, a math sheet, and I have to write a poem."

"Well, why don't you get started," suggested Dan.

"Okay," replied Hannah. "Where should I do my homework, Daddy?"

"There's a nice desk in one of the little front rooms," said Rachel. "Why don't we set you up there? Come on. I'll show you."

"Okay!" cried Hannah and she followed Rachel out of the kitchen.

They passed through the dining room and the living room into the front hall. On either side of the hall was a small room. In one was an old wicker sofa with a small table next to it. In one corner was a tall maple cabinet painted robin's egg blue inside and holding a shell collection. The other room had a pretty little pine desk and chair, a bookcase, and a comfortable looking overstuffed armchair upholstered in a faded fabric with huge pink roses on it.

"What funny little rooms," said Hannah. "Why do you suppose they made them?"

"Well, I think I remember Mrs. Harrington, the lady who used to own this house, saying that these two rooms were originally part of the porch. At some point they closed them in. I think maybe they wanted places where they could sit and look at the water during the colder winter months."

"I think they're neat," said Hannah, "and I think I'll do very good work in here," she continued, running her hand over the smooth surface of the pine desk.

"Good," said Rachel. "Why don't you get your backpack and you can get started."

"Thank you Mrs.—Rachel, for everything," said Hannah softly. "My Dad seemed so happy when he picked me up today. It's been a long time since he's been happy. He worries so much, but for once, he doesn't seem worried at all."

"Well, I'm glad of that," said Rachel. "And I don't want you worrying either."

"Oh, I hardly ever worry. I believe in having a positive attitude."

Hannah had no idea why Rachel suddenly burst out laughing.

21

By the time Hannah arrived home from school on Thursday, Rachel had transformed the dingy little apartment into a warm and inviting home. The living room area was painted a rich cream and there was the old wicker sofa from the house with plump cushions and two comfortable if mismatched chairs. An old trunk served as a coffee table and two upturned barrels draped with pretty cloths held table lamps that Rachel had found in a closet. An old fashioned braided rug covered most of the linoleum floor. The windows had lengths of rich green fabric draped artfully over rods. Sheer white curtains provided a bit of privacy. A small square table and four chairs fit nicely into the kitchen area which was painted a cheerful yellow. Yellow and white gingham curtains were at the window. Dan's room was a soothing shade of blue. Rachel had furnished the room with a simple wooden bed with a blue and white quilt and an old oak dresser. A chair and ottoman in a corner with a standing lamp created a cozy place to sit and read, and several table lamps provided warm lighting. Another old braided rug covered the floor.

"It's beautiful," cried Hannah as she surveyed Rachel's handiwork. "How did you do all this?"

"Well, I found the local thrift shop and they had a lot of these things. I also did some exploring in my own house where I found a lot of the lamps and things. Come on, I want to show you your room," said Rachel. She took the little girl by the hand and led her to the entrance of the little alcove, now partitioned by a wooden folding screen. "No door, but the screen will give you some privacy," suggested Rachel as she walked around the screen into the little bedroom she had created for Hannah.

A white iron bedstead, covered in a soft pink and white quilt, stood in one corner, a white painted table with a glass lamp stood beside it. A tall cupboard for her clothes was placed against the far wall and under the window, where Hannah could look out and see a tiny patch of ocean, was the little pine desk that had been in the front room of *Windswept*. Organdy curtains crisscrossed the window, and a soft green rug covered the floor. A small bookcase stood in front of the screen. But it was the beautiful deep rose walls that made the room.

"I hope you like the color," said Rachel. "I know it's a strong color, but I thought the contrast was so nice. And honestly, it just makes me feel so happy."

"Oh Rachel—it's the most beautiful room I've ever seen. Is it really, truly for me?" she asked as she lovingly touched each item in the room.

"Yes, Hannah, it's really, truly for you. I'm so glad you like it!" Rachel turned to find Dan standing in the entrance to the little room.

"I don't know how to thank you, Rachel," he said. "All I've ever wanted was to give my baby a decent place to live and a chance at a better life than the one I've had. You're like an angel, come straight from Heaven. I can never repay you for all you've done."

"Yes, you can," replied Rachel. "You can be the best general contractor this island has ever seen and you can love that little girl just as you do, for always. That's all the repayment I need," she laughed. "Now, I believe there are still some of those oatmeal cookies left. After that, you can start unloading that van and settle in. I'm expecting you for supper tonight, but tomorrow you can fend for yourselves—so there!"

22

Dan and Hannah were all settled and living quite independently of Rachel when the twins arrived with Gommy and Gompy for Christmas. In fact, there were days when she saw only a brief glimpse of Hannah. Dan she saw daily as he worked with her and the builders to refine the plans in anticipation of starting the renovations.

It was the Friday before Christmas and Rachel began watching the road and listening for the sound of Gompy's car a half hour before the ferry carrying her children was even due in Vineyard Haven. Thankfully planning the renovations had kept her busy during the long three week separation, but the nights were still long and lonely. She was overjoyed at the prospect of spending two weeks with her children.

She had decorated the tree the night before and now it shimmered with tinsel and tiny white lights. She had brought the boxes of ornaments with her when she had returned from her last trip to New Jersey. It had been bittersweet unwrapping each ornament and finding just the right spot for it. So many of the ornaments had a special story or memory attached to it.

When she and Ben had first been married, they had no Christmas ornaments of their own. They'd been living in Brooklyn then and didn't have much money for extras. One night as Rachel was walking home from the subway, she had passed by the local wine shop. In a large box left for the garbage men, she had seen dozens of gold plastic decorations used to adorn gift packages of wine. She asked in the store if they were throwing them away. The old gentleman who ran the store assured her that they were for the trash, so Rachel asked if she might have them. He gave her a quizzical look, but agreed that Rachel might have the plastic decorations. So Ben and Rachel's first Christmas tree was decorated with discarded plastic gewgaws from the wine shop and strings of cranberries and popcorn. As the years went by, the plastic ornaments had been replaced with newer ones, but they kept two or three of them as a memento of their first years together.

Beneath the tree were dozens of gaily wrapped packages. Rachel knew she had probably spent more than she should have, but somehow, this first Christmas without Ben, she felt it was all right. As she looked at the tree, her breath caught and she felt the sting of tears. "Oh, Ben—my sweet Ben. Are you here with me now? I hope so. I miss you so much. I don't know how I am going to make it through Christmas without you."

"You'll do just fine," a voice said behind her and she turned, startled, to see Gompy standing in the door. He opened his arms to her and she went to him. He held her for a moment as she fought back the tears.

"I didn't think I was speaking out loud," she whispered.

"It's all right, Rachel," soothed Gompy. "It's what we're all thinking. It's why I came in ahead of the kids."

"Are they having a hard time?" she asked worriedly.

"Well, they're awfully quiet. Gommy tried to get a carol sing going in the car, and Sam broke down. After that, she and Andy just looked out the window. Andy didn't even pig out when we stopped at McDonalds."

"Well," laughed Rachel, "that is serious!"

"I'm sure they'll be better now that they're here," said Gompy.

"Mom? Mom? We're here!" cried Andy as he barreled through the door with Sam right behind. Before she knew it, Rachel's arms were full of her children, and they were all laughing and crying at once.

"Oh my gosh, let me look at you!" cried Rachel, holding the twins at arm's length.

"Oh, Mom, don't be silly. It's only been three weeks!" protested Sam.

"Three long weeks for me," Rachel responded.

"Us, too," agreed Andy.

"I could use a little help here!"

"Gommy!" exclaimed Rachel. "Why are you carrying those heavy bags?"

"It seemed better than spending Christmas in the car!!"

"Andy, Sam—get those bags away from your grandmother at once. You know where everybody's room is, so just put the bags where they belong," ordered Rachel as she bent to pick up Andy's bookbag from the floor. "Good Heavens, Andrew—what have you got in this bookbag," she groaned, "bricks?"

"Noooo Moooom," drawled Andy, "not bricks—books."

"Excuse me? Books? Getting you to read is like getting a cat to take a bath. What sort of books?"

"I read when I'm interested in the subject," protested Andy.

"And what has you so intrigued, I wonder. Mind if I have a peek?" asked Rachel.

"Be my guest," shrugged Andy.

Rachel unzipped the backpack and began pulling out books, one by one.

"*Pirates of Cape Cod, Pirate Legends, Blackbeard.* I'm sensing a theme here."

"Well, if we're going to hunt pirate treasure, I thought I should be well informed!"

"I think that's great, kiddo. Now, how about taking this *library* up stairs along with the other bags?"

"Come on, A," said Sam as she grabbed a large valise and headed up the stairs. Andy followed with his bag of books and another suitcase. Rachel turned to her mother-in-law.

"Oh, Gommy, I'm so glad you and Gompy are here!" said Rachel as she gave her mother-in-law a warm hug.

"We're awfully glad to be here, too. I can't imagine having Christmas without you—especially—" her voice broke and she took a deep breath, "especially this year."

"I know, I know," said Rachel and now it was her turn to offer comfort. As hard as it was for her to have lost Ben, she could not begin to imagine the loss of a child. "But Gompy is right. We're going to get through this. We have to for the children's sake and because that's what Ben would have wanted."

"You're right, dear," said Gommy as she dabbed at her eyes with a hanky. "He'd be scolding me this very moment if he were here! Oh, look at your tree. It's a beauty. And all those presents. Is there anything left in the stores?"

"Not much," laughed Rachel.

A cough interrupted her and she turned to see Dan standing in the door.

"I'm sorry to intrude, Rachel, but Middleton just called and he needs an answer on that roof for the side porch before he puts his lumber order in."

"Oh, Dan, come in. Come in. You remember my in-laws?" asked Rachel.

"Sure do. Nice to see you both again. Rachel sure has been looking forward to your arrival."

"Well, the feeling is mutual," replied Gompy. "And we're very grateful to you for the help you've been giving Rachel on the renovations. From everything she's told us, it's going to be terrific."

"I think she has a good honest builder, and I'll make sure that the work is done right. It's the least I can do for all she's done for me and Hannah."

"Oh, we're so looking forward to meeting Hannah. Especially the children. Rachel has told them all about her. She sounds delightful."

"She's a sweetheart, that's for sure," responded Dan. "I guess you'll meet her tonight at the holiday concert."

"Oh, I forgot to tell you," said Rachel as Gommy looked puzzled. "Hannah is in a special program at her school tonight. She's going to read a poem she wrote and she wants us all to come. I thought it would be a nice way to get the holidays started."

"It sounds wonderful," said Gommy, "but if we're going out, I'd better take a little nap now, or I'll be asleep half-way through."

"I'll join you," said Gompy. "We'll see you later, Dan."

"Yes, sir. Look forward to it."

After Gommy and Gompy had gone up the stairs, Rachel turned to Dan. "So what do you think about the roof over the side porch?"

"Well, I think it's pretty expensive, because they have to tie into the existing rafters. And you'll lose a good bit of light which will make that end of this room awful dark."

"That's exactly what I was thinking," said Rachel. "I think we'll skip the roof. I'd rather spend the money elsewhere. Will you call Middleton and let him know my decision."

"You bet. Thanks. I'll see you later. Seven-thirty."

"We'll be there."

Dan hurried out through the side door as the twins came bounding down the stairs.

"We'll be where?" they chorused.

"Hannah's school. They're doing a special holiday program tonight and she asked if we would come."

"Cool. I can't wait to meet her," cried Sam.

"Wish she had been a boy," grumbled Andy.

"Well, I'm sure you'll like her anyway. She's very pretty."

"Aw, who cares if she's pretty? Can she play basketball?"

"I don't know, but with two MVP athletes to teach her, I think she'll learn pretty quickly. By the way, have I told you both how proud I am of you winning those awards?"

"Only about a hundred times," teased Andy. "I sure wish you could have been at the awards ceremonies."

"I do, too, honey. But it seemed sort of perfect somehow that Sam took Gompy to her father-daughter dinner and you took Gommy to your mother-son dinner."

"Yeah, I guess you're right," agreed Andy reluctantly. "Still, I wish you and Dad could have been there with us."

"They were," said Sam. "Mom and Dad are always with us—" her voice caught. She took a breath. "Nope—no way. I am not going to cry. I'm not spending my whole vacation crying. Dad would have wanted us to celebrate, so I say, let's get started."

"That's right," agreed Rachel. "You have to—"

"Have a positive attitude!" they shouted together.

23

The Oak Bluffs School was festooned with holiday decorations as Rachel, the children, and Gommy and Gompy joined the crowd moving through the glass doors into the lobby.

"Wow! This is very cool!" exclaimed Sam as she looked around the modern building. "It's so different from Williams Street. It must be really new. I hope our school looks like this."

"It is pretty new I think," said Rachel. "It's beautiful—so light and open. And this will be your school come September."

"What?" cried Andy. "Mom, we're supposed to go to middle school— we're done with elementary school!"

"I know that, silly. But the Vineyard schools are K to Eight schools. You'll be in this building for the next three years, and then you go to the regional high school. "

"Phew! I was afraid I had to stay back a year or something!"

They all admired the art work adorning the walls as they passed down the long hall towards the auditorium. There was already a large crowd and they hurried to find five seats together. They waved to Dan who was seated in a special section reserved for the parents of the students.

After a few minutes, the lights dimmed and the members of the student orchestra filed in to take their places. The program began with a medley of holiday songs played by the orchestra, and then the curtains parted to reveal the student chorus. Everyone applauded as the music teacher stepped to the center of the stage to introduce the program. Each grade performed several musical pieces with one or two students reading poems and stories they had written on the theme of "The Greatest Gift". When it was time for the fourth graders to perform, they sang a Christmas carol, a Hanukah song, and a Brazilian folk song. Then Hannah, dressed in a beautiful red velvet dress with her hair tied back in a dark green ribbon, stepped to the front of the stage. She took a deep breath and spoke loudly and clearly.

"Mrs. Brown, my teacher, asked us to write a poem about *The Greatest Gift*. I would like to read mine for you now." She took a deep breath and began:

My Greatest Gift
by Hannah Furman

Our Father, who art in Heaven
Thank you for the gift you've given
For the strong arms that hold me in the night
When I wake from a nightmare, full of fright
For the smile that brightens every day
And the ears that listen to all I say
For the eyes that sometimes fill with tears
For the heart that has loved me for all these years
Thank you for the greatest gift I've ever had
Thank you, dear Father, for the gift of my dad.

As she finished reciting, Hannah looked down at Dan and blew him a kiss. There was a moment of absolute silence, and then the audience began to applaud. As Rachel looked over at Sam and Andy, she saw that they had been moved by Hannah's poem and that a bond had formed between her children and Dan's daughter. She closed her eyes and thought of Ben, her greatest gift, and then looked again at her children and realized yet again, that he lived on in them.

After the concert, everyone was invited to share punch and cookies provided by the parents. Dan's face lit up as he saw Hannah working her way through the crowd to him. He hugged her tightly, and she hugged him back. Suddenly both were weeping and laughing at the same time.

"Thank you, Hannah," whispered Dan. "That is the most beautiful gift I have ever received. I will try to live up to all the things you said."

"You already do, Daddy. That's why I wrote it," responded Hannah. She turned to Rachel. "Did you like it, Rachel?"

"Oh yes, very much, Hannah. It was wonderful," assured Rachel. She paused, and then drew Sam and Andy to her. "Hannah, these are my children, Sam and Andy. This is Hannah."

"Hi!" said Sam, smiling and holding out her hand.

"Hi," said Hannah as she shook the proffered hand.

Sam gently pulled Hannah to her in a hug. "Thank you for the poem. It's exactly what I would have said about our dad—Mom, too!"

"Hey! What about me?" asked Andy.

"Oh yeah—this is my brother—Andy. He's not bad—for a boy!" teased Sam.

"We've heard a lot about you," said Andy as he shook Hannah's hand. Then, without a breath, "Can anybody have those cookies?"

As the adult's laughter subsided, the three children headed for the refreshments.

"I think you two are going to have your hands full," said Gompy.

"What do you mean 'going to'?" laughed Dan.

24

Christmas morning dawned cold and crisp with a clear and sunny sky. As Sam and Andy tumbled down the stairs, they were greeted by the aroma of bacon cooking and coffee cake warming. Gommy and Gompy were already in the living room sipping coffee; and as the twins shouted a chorus of "Merry Christmas!" Rachel came in from the kitchen carrying a tray laden with coffee cake and crisp bacon; the Bennett's traditional Christmas breakfast.

As each of them chose a seat and settled in, Rachel distributed plates and napkins and then unpinned the stockings. Just hours before, the stockings had hung empty and limp from the mantle, but now they were stuffed to overflowing. The next hour was filled with ooh's and ah's as everything from colored pencils to hair pins was exclaimed over as if they were the rarest of treasures. When the last tissue wrapped surprise had been opened, the celebrants carried their gifts up to their rooms and changed into daytime clothes from their pajamas.

When everyone was gathered again in the living room, Rachel and Gompy began to distribute the gifts from under the tree. Sam and Andy were delighted with their Martha's Vineyard sweat shirts, and Gommy and Gompy looked forward to using their gift certificates at The Bunch of Grapes Bookstore. Everyone had a beautiful new sweater knitted by Gommy, and Rachel was thrilled with a gift certificate to a linen catalogue that would mean new sheets and quilts for all the *Windswept* beds. When all the gifts had been opened, the twins exchanged secretive looks and Sam turned to Gompy.

"Can you help us, Gomps?" she asked.

"You bet," cried Gompy enthusiastically.

"Help you with what?" inquired Rachel.

"You'll see," answered Andy as the twins and their Grandfather went out the side door.

"Do you know what's going on, Gommy?" asked Rachel.

"Not a clue," assured Gommy, smiling broadly.

"Hmmm—very mysterious," laughed Rachel. The door opened and Gompy and the twins returned carrying a large rectangular package, wrapped in Christmas paper. They set it down in front of Rachel, and she looked at the twins in surprise as she read the card aloud.

Dear Mom,

We weren't sure what to give you for Christmas. We knew this would be a hard one for all of us. We asked Gommy and Gompy about our idea, and they thought it was a good one. We hope you will, too. We know it might make you cry and we're sorry, but we think eventually it will make you smile.

We love you so much Mommy, and we know how lonely it must be for you missing Dad and with us far away in New Jersey. Maybe this will help.

Love,

Sam and Andy

"Well, I am mystified," Rachel admitted. "Can I open it now?"

"Sure!"

Carefully, Rachel unwrapped the package. As the paper fell away, she gasped and looked at her children as a tear rolled down her cheek.

"I knew it," cried Andy, punching Sam in the arm. "We made her cry!"

"It's okay, sweetheart," whispered Rachel, truly unable to speak as she let her eyes rest on the painting in front of her; a painting of her beloved Ben and the twins. The likenesses were remarkable, right down to the twinkle in Ben's eyes. "How—where?" she stammered.

"Mrs. Morris, the art teacher at Williams Street, told us about this artist friend of hers who painted portraits from photographs. We picked this one because it was of all three of us here at the beach. Do you like it?"

A great sob burst from Rachel as she hugged the twins tightly to her and whispered, "Yes, yes, oh yes, I do."

"Gommy and Gompy paid for the frame, so it's from them, too."

Rachel went to her in-laws and hugged them both. Then to everyone's surprise, she began to laugh.

"What's so funny, Mom?" asked Andy.

"You'll see."

Rachel left the room and returned a moment later with three wrapped boxes. She handed one each to the twins and the third to Gommy and Gompy.

"I guess great minds kind of think alike," she said. As they all looked at her in confusion, she said, "Go on—open them."

They did, and each found a beautiful leather bound album. Rachel was not the only one who shed tears as they looked through the collection of photographs that Rachel had assembled for each of them. She had spent hours selecting the pictures for the albums that chronicled their lives with Ben. Gommy and Gompy's began with a photo of Gommy holding the newly born Ben in the hospital, and the twins' showed Ben holding <u>them</u> on the day <u>they</u> were born. There were pictures of birthdays and Christmases, anniversary parties, soccer and basketball games. Each album was different and for the next hour, they sat and looked at the pictures recalling wonderful times spent with Ben. There were some tears to be sure, but more laughter than anything, which is what Rachel had hoped for. Rachel, meanwhile, took down the seascape print that she had hung over the fireplace and replaced it with the painting of Ben and the twins.

As she stood back to look at it, she alternated between a quiet happiness at the sight of Ben and her children and a cold emptiness. She realized, not for the first time, that Christmas would be like this from now on—pleasant, but without joy. "Like a Christmas tree without lights," she thought.

She turned back to her family.

"All right, you guys, we have company coming for dinner, and there's a lot of work to do, so let's get moving!"

The next few hours were busy with table setting, turkey preparation and the thousand other tasks that go into a big family dinner. When Dan and Hannah and Em Michaels arrived late that afternoon, the house was filled with the aroma of roasting turkey, and the dining room was awash in the glow of candles and the scent of the bayberry center piece. The table was laden with all the accompaniments of a Christmas feast from little cups of salted nuts to chocolate Santas. As the bird was ceremoniously brought in, everyone applauded.

"This is amazing, Rachel," complimented Dan.

"It sure beats last Christmas, doesn't it Daddy?" added Hannah. Dan looked serious for a moment, but didn't speak. He just nodded.

"Why?" asked Andy. "What did you do last Christmas?"

"We ate at a church. It was kind of depressing. Plus, they had ham!"

"Yuck!"

"That must have been very hard for you, Dan," Gommy said gently, seeing the look on Dan's face.

"It was. It's hard to believe how much better this Christmas has been; a nice place to live, a job, and new friends to share the day with. I can't thank you all enough for the way you've helped us out." He paused. "It made me want to help somebody else, so I've volunteered with *Habitat for Humanity* to help build some houses for people here on the island who need a place to live."

"Oh, Dan, what a wonderful thing to do!" cried Rachel.

"Seemed little enough — plus, my work will count towards Hannah and me getting a *Habitat* house of our own someday. And I promise it won't interfere with my work here."

"The thought never occurred to me," assured Rachel. "Now, who's ready for pie and ice cream?"

25

The last morning of the twins' holiday visit dawned cold and gray. As Sam stood at her bedroom window and looked out at the steel gray water, she silently said a little prayer that a blizzard would suddenly materialize. She dreaded going home and having to say goodbye, yet again, to her mother. She knew that it would only be six months until she would return for good, but just at this moment, six months seemed like a lifetime to Sam.

There was a gentle tapping on her door.

"Sam—you up?" Andy whispered.

"Sure—come in."

The door swung open and Andy's head of uncombed hair appeared around it. One look at his face told Sam that she was not alone in her feelings. She held her arms open, and they were filled with the boy who shared so much with her. Sam truly believed that she and Andy were simply two halves of the same person, so alike were they and so in tune emotionally.

"I don't want to go, Sam," Andy admitted. "Why can't we just stay here? The house is good enough for us to live in and we can go to school here—I don't see why Mom wants us to go back to New Jersey."

"She doesn't <u>want</u> us to go, you goof. She just thinks it's best for us to finish the school year at Williams Street. Don't you want to be there for graduation with all our friends?"

"I guess so, but I think I'd rather be here with Mom if I could choose."

"Me, too, I guess. But in this case, I don't think we get to."

"Don't get to what?" asked Rachel as she came through the door with a pile of clean laundry.

"Oh, nothing," stammered Sam.

"Don't play poker, kiddo," laughed Rachel. "What's up?"

"We don't want to go home!" Andy blurted out.

"Oh, buddy, I don't want you to go either," said Rachel as she gathered both children to her. "I would love nothing more than for you to stay, but you need to finish the school year so you don't fall behind. Besides, there's so much work to be done on the house to make it ready."

"We don't care about the house," protested Sam.

"And we promise we'll study twice as hard to make sure we don't miss anything," promised Andy.

"Guys, it's only six months."

"Six months is a long time, Mom," argued Sam. "A lot can happen in six months—a lot of bad stuff."

"What do you mean?" asked Rachel. "What kind of bad stuff? Nothing bad is going to happen."

"Like nothing bad happened to Daddy?" said Andy.

Suddenly the room was deathly still.

"No, something bad did happen to Daddy," whispered Rachel, "but that doesn't mean that something bad is going to happen to you or to me. The last thing Daddy would have wanted would be for us to live in fear for the rest of our lives. The men who killed Daddy and all those other people wanted us to be afraid. They wanted us to change what we do, to give up things we want, out of fear. If we do that, they win and Daddy died for nothing. I won't do that."

"I hate those men," hissed Andy. "I hate them more than anything in the whole world."

"Daddy wouldn't want you to hate anyone, Andy. It doesn't help to hate them. It was hate that made those men do what they did."

"I can't help it. It's the way I feel!" cried Andy.

"I hope someday your feelings will change. The only way Daddy's death can have meaning is if we become the best people we can be and do wonderful things with our lives."

"But why can't we do those wonderful things here with you?" asked Sam. "Why do we have to go back?"

Rachel was silent. To be honest, she wasn't sure herself why they had to go home. They could stay. The house was certainly livable. She was sure Gommy and Gompy wouldn't mind. She had overheard Gommy telling Gompy that she wished they could go to Florida for the winter as they usually did. She could put the house on the market, and the kids could start school here. Suddenly, sending them home made no sense. They were miserable about it and so was she.

"Well, I may be nuts—but okay."

"Okay what?" asked Sam.

"Okay, you can stay."

The shrieking and shouting and hugging and crying was so loud that Gommy ran up the stairs and burst through the door thinking that something awful had happened. By the time she arrived on the scene, however, all three of them were flopped on the bed laughing joyously.

"What on earth?" Gommy stammered.

"How would you and Gompy like to spend the winter in Florida?" asked Rachel.

"Florida? You're sending the children to Florida? I don't understand."

"No—of course you don't. I'm sorry, Gommy. I skipped one important piece of information. The kids aren't going home. They're going to stay here with me. You and Gompy are off the hook. You can go to Florida and bask in the sun while the three of us freeze to death in this uninsulated house!"

"Well, it's about time!"

"What?" asked Rachel in a shocked voice.

"Gompy and I have always felt that the children would be happier with you. I mean, we understood that for a while it was easier for you to leave them with us, and Heaven knows, we loved every minute of our time with them, but you were clearly unhappy being apart from them and they were certainly miserable without you. Children belong with their mother. Whatever little hardships they might have to endure until the house is finished don't matter. They need to be with you and you need to be with them. And, yes, Gompy and I would love to go to Florida for the winter—so it all works out for everybody."

Within the hour, the car was packed, and Gommy and Gompy were ready to go.

"I don't think there's any way I can ever thank you for all you've done for me—for us," whispered Rachel as she hugged Gompy tightly. "Ben was so lucky to have you for parents, and he inherited so much of your loving kindness."

"My dear girl—Ben was the love of our lives and you were the love of his. We take comfort knowing that Ben lives on in his children and in the love you have for him. It is we who are grateful to you for allowing us to help. I don't know what we would have done if you had just packed up and gone away."

"None of our lives will ever be the same," continued Gommy, "but as long as we can share the memory of Ben's love and celebrate his life in the accomplishments of his children, we will never truly have to let him go. We love you,

Rachel. You were a blessing in Ben's life and a blessing in ours." Tears traced a course along the lines in Gommy's face; lines which had grown deeper in the last few months. "Now, we'd best be on our way or we'll miss the boat."

"Call us when you get home so we know you're there safely," said Rachel. The twins smothered their grandparents in hugs and kisses, knowing it might be many months before they had the chance to be with them again.

"We will! And you two behave and help your mother!" cried Gompy as he backed the car out of the drive. Rachel and the twins stood in the middle of the bluff road waving until the car turned the bend by the lighthouse and disappeared.

"Well, as long as you're here, I guess I'd better put you to work! There are beds to be changed!"

The twins groaned theatrically as the happy trio nearly skipped up the path and into the house that suddenly really did seem like home.

26

"Gosh it's huge! It didn't seem this big at Christmas," whispered Sam as Rachel and the children pushed through the front door of the Oak Bluffs School a few days later.

"That's because it's a K to Eight school. Remember, you'll be here until you go to high school," Rachel reminded them.

"There's the office," said Andy pointing to a door that opened into the school lobby. "What's that word under *office?*"

"I think it's Portuguese," said Rachel.

"Why?" asked Sam.

"There's a large Portuguese speaking population on the island. Mostly Brazilian, now, I think, although many of the original sailors who came here to be part of the whaling industry came from Cape Verde and the Azores. They spoke Portuguese, too."

"Cool!" exclaimed Sam. "Maybe I can learn to speak Portuguese!"

They entered the office and approached the front desk. A pleasant looking woman glanced up.

"Good morning. Can I help you?"

"I hope so," replied Rachel. "I'm Rachel Bennett and these are my twins, Samantha and Andrew. We've just moved here from New Jersey and I'd like to enroll them in school. They are both in the fifth grade."

"Well, welcome to the Vineyard and to Oak Bluffs School. I'm Helen Sanders, the school secretary. What brought you to the island?"

"My dad bought us a house here before he—" Sam stopped a moment, "before he was killed on nine-eleven," she finished.

"We decided he would have wanted us to live here because we all love it so much," added Andy.

The woman at the desk looked at Rachel and said quietly, "What a terrible ordeal you've been through. I'm so sorry—for all of you. I hope the Vineyard will turn out to be a haven for you."

"Thank you. You're most kind."

"Well, now, let's see what we have to do to get these two youngsters registered." She pushed away from her desk and crossed the room to another office door. "Larry," she called through the open door, "could you come out here a moment? We have two new students."

"Right-o—I'm on my way" called a jovial sounding man. A moment later, a tall, impossibly thin man with bright red curly hair appeared. He was wearing khaki pants, a tweed jacket, and a bright orange shirt with a green bow tie. Andy and Sam nearly laughed out loud as the man practically leapt through the door and bounded over to where they were waiting with Rachel. The man stretched out his hand to Rachel.

"Larry Binzen," he cried as if he were announcing the center ring attraction at the circus. "Principal of the Oak Bluffs School. Welcome, welcome, welcome. And who are these two fine looking young people?"

"Samantha Bennett," replied Sam extending her hand to shake the principal's as she had been taught. "And this is my brother Andrew. I prefer to be called Sam and Andrew is generally known as Andy. We're twins."

"You don't say. You don't look much alike!" Mr. Binzen exclaimed, laughing at his little joke. "And you must be Mrs. Bennett!"

"Yes. I'm happy to meet you Mr. Binzen."

"My pleasure entirely. Why don't you all step into my office, and we'll get this process underway. Just follow me. Helen, would you bring me two of our finest orientation packets for these young people and a Parent Information folder for Mrs. Bennett? Right this way, now folks. Right this way."

An hour later, having filled out dozens of forms and holding several more to be completed by the children's pediatrician and their former principal, Rachel gave both her children a kiss and a hug, much to Andy's embarrassment, and pushed back through the main door to the building as Mrs. Sanders led Sam and Andy up a flight of stairs to introduce them to their new teachers.

"Sam, maybe this wasn't such a good idea after all," whispered Andy. "I'm scared."

"Me, too, but we'll be fine. I'll meet you in the cafeteria at lunch. Hang in there till then—and remember—"

"I know," interrupted Andy. "Have a positive attitude!"

27

By the time Andy and Sam met up in the cafeteria, they had both formed strong opinions about their new school. As they carried their trays to one of the tables, they both began talking at once.

"My teacher is so cool. He used to be a marine and now he's in the reserves. He coaches the basketball team at the high school, and he has six kids!" exclaimed Andy.

"Six kids!" exclaimed Sam. "That's a whole basketball team plus a sub."

"Except one of them is a girl," replied Andy.

"And what does that have to do with it? As I recall, I was the MVP in my soccer league. Girls make great athletes!"

"Okay, okay Miss Feminist. I admit some girls can play sports, but basketball is really a guy's game."

"Obviously you have not been paying attention to the WNBA, and it's MS. Feminist if you please."

"What's your teacher like?" asked Andy changing the subject.

"She's nice. Mrs. McDonough. She really likes math, and she read us this cool story about a train that disappeared because the track was really this thing called a Mobius strip. Then she showed us how to make one."

"What's a Mobius Strip?"

"It's a one-sided piece of paper. I'll show you later," assured Sam at Andy's confused expression." Listen, do you mind if I skip out? I want to talk to one of the girls in my class over there."

"No, that's cool. I'm going to go outside and shoot some hoops."

"It's the middle of winter!"

"So?" laughed Andy as he grabbed his tray and headed for the cart that held the used trays.

Sam returned her tray and then moved over to another table where several girls from her class were eating.

"Hey, Sam. Sit," said a pretty brunette named Katie Clark." We were just saying how nice it is to have another girl in the class."

"Yeah, I noticed there are a lot more boys than girls."

"Too many," quipped Lucy Vandermade and the others laughed.

"It seems like a nice class though," Sam observed.

"It is," said Katie. "I think it's the nicest class I've been in. So where do you live?"

"I live on the bluff road in East Chop," said Sam.

"Wow—you must be loaded," exclaimed Ann Garner, a studious looking girl with glasses that could not hide the twinkle of fun in her eyes.

"No—anything but," Sam replied.

"Those houses on the bluff are expensive—and I didn't think they were winterized," continued Ann.

"They're not, mostly. We're renovating the house."

"How did you end up here?" asked Katie.

"Well, my dad bought the house for my mom for their fifteenth wedding anniversary and then when he—" she faltered, "when he died, we all decided that he would want us to live here."

"Gosh, I'm sorry about your dad—that's awful. How did he die?" asked Lucy.

"Lucy!" cried Katie, horrified that her friend would ask such a direct question.

"What?" queried Lucy, not understanding her friend's disapproval.

"It's okay," said Sam quietly. "My dad was in the North Tower of the World Trade Center on nine-eleven. That's how he died."

There was a long and uncomfortable silence, and then Katie reached across the table and covered Sam's hand with hers. "That's so sad. It must be awful. I'm so sorry."

"Thanks. It is sad—and weird," admitted Sam. "Kids never imagine that they might not have their parents around forever. You don't realize how much a part of your life they are until they're not around."

"Yeah—" whispered Ann.

"Ann's mom has been sick—breast cancer," explained Katie.

"But she's doing better, right Annie?" asked Lucy.

"Yes, thank goodness. She just had her one year check-up, and everything was perfect. But it was so scary when she was in the hospital and everything—when I thought she might—"

"That almost seems worse to me," said Sam understanding her new friend's feelings. "My dad died so unexpectedly. One day he was here and then he was gone. I didn't have to worry about losing him."

"Mrs. Mc Donough said you had a brother," said Katie to change the subject and the mood.

Sam groaned dramatically, "Yeah—Andy—he's in the other fifth grade. We're twins," she explained.

"Wow, that's cool. I always wanted a twin sister," admitted Lucy.

"That's all we need—two Lucy's," teased Ann. "Is it true what they say about twins? Do you guys, like, know what the other is thinking?"

"Actually, we do," said Sam. "We're very different in many ways, but we do seem to know how the other is feeling without being told. Andy can be a pest, but I love him—especially since my dad died. Andy looks a lot like Daddy, but he has my mom's personality. I'm more like my dad."

"Whoa—there's the bell. We'd better get back," urged Katie as the lunch room began to empty.

Sam smiled as she walked with her classmates. "Maybe this will be okay," she thought to herself.

•••

A few hours later, Sam met Andy at the front door and they headed out to the parking lot to find their Mom's car.

"I don't see her," said Andy. There was a fleeting look of panic on his face.

"Don't worry, she'll be here. She probably just got caught up in her errands or something," said Sam to soothe him.

Just then they heard a male voice calling their names. They looked toward the voice and saw Dan standing by his van. They crossed the parking lot to him.

"Hop in," he said. "Your Mom had an appointment, and I said I would pick you guys up when I came for Hannah."

Dan slid open the door to the rear seat and Sam and Andy climbed in behind Hannah, who was already in the front. She turned eagerly and asked, "How was your first day? Whose class are you in?"

"I'm in Mrs. McDonough's class," replied Sam smiling. She and Andy were both very fond of Hannah.

"I'm in Mr. Hazlet's class. He's really cool. He has six kids!" cried Andy.

"I know. His son, Tim, is in my class," replied Hannah. "Tim is really nice and super smart in science. He's always building machines and they actually work."

"Cool!"

"What kind of appointment did Mom have, Dan?" asked Sam. "She didn't mention it this morning."

"She didn't really say. She said she'd be home around four and you should do your homework 'cause you're going to the movies tonight."

"Oh yeah—I forgot," cried Andy excited at the prospect. "Hey, can Hannah come, too?" he asked.

"Can I Daddy?"

"I don't see why not—as long as you get your homework done. I've got some paper work to catch up on, so I might appreciate a little peace and quiet!"

"Oh boy—what movie are you going to?" asked Hannah, not that she really cared.

"*Harry Potter and the Sorcerer's Stone,*" cried Sam. "I hope it's as good as the book."

"I bet it will be good, but I don't think it could ever be as good as the book," said Andy.

"I never thought I would hear you say anything good about a book," laughed Sam.

"This one is different—I don't know why—it just is," insisted Andy.

"I agree," replied Dan from the front seat. "I've never been much of a reader, myself, but I read the first one to Hannah and I was hooked. I think I was more excited than she was when we heard the new one was coming out."

"You should hear Daddy read aloud. He does all these different voices and stuff. It's almost like seeing a movie, only it's just in your head."

"That's neat. Maybe you should be an actor," suggested Andy.

"Actually, Daddy has been an actor. He was in a holiday show that the Island Theater Workshop put on last year. They do one every year and they use islanders to play all the roles. There are always a lot of kids in them, too. Next year I want to audition for it. I think it would be so fun to be in a play."

"Well, your acting career will have to wait till your homework is done, sweetie. Here we are. Everybody get to work, so you can go to the movie later," urged Dan as the kids piled out of the van. "Rachel left some cookies for you in the kitchen, and there's milk in the fridge."

Sam and Andy let Hannah and Dan go ahead. "Where do you think Mom is?" asked Andy.

"I have no idea. She didn't say anything about not picking us up when she left us this morning, so either it was a last minute appointment or she didn't want to say anything about it."

"You don't think she's sick or anything, do you?" asked Andy in a worried tone.

"Don't start imagining things, kiddo. She would have told us if she was sick. You know Mom doesn't keep secrets. It's probably something about the house. Now come on—let's get a cookie and get to homework. I want to see that movie."

A short time later, Rachel's car pulled into the driveway. Andy ran down the stairs three at a time and launched himself off the small side porch as Rachel came around the front of the car.

"Whoa, there, buddy. Where's the fire?" laughed Rachel.

"Where have you been? Are you okay? You're not sick are you? Sam said you would tell us if you were sick," blurted Andy.

"Hold on, there. Calm down," cautioned Rachel as Sam came down the steps with a worried expression. Rachel shook her head and smiled. "I'm fine. I'm not sick. I had an appointment."

"What kind of appointment?" demanded Andy.

"Well, if you must know, I went on a job interview," replied Rachel. She couldn't repress a chuckle at the look of astonishment that washed over Andy's face.

"A job interview?" asked Sam as she joined her mother and Andy.

"Yes—a job interview. We need some income, you know. The money we get from selling the house in Jersey will hopefully pay for the renovations, but we have a mortgage and it will be expensive to run this big old house—to say nothing of feeding the two of you! Do you have any idea how much you eat?" laughed Rachel.

"Well, Mom, did you get the job?" asked Sam.

"I did."

"Mom — come on," demanded Andy. "What kind of job did you get?"

"I've been hired to work with an interior decorating firm in Edgartown."

"Wow! That's cool. How come they hired *you?*" asked Andy.

"Gee thanks, Andy. You make it sound like they've lost their minds!" laughed Rachel.

"Uh—no—gee—gosh, Mom, I didn't..." he stuttered.

"That's all right. Before you guys were born, I worked for one of the biggest fabric houses in New York, so I have some good experience. It's just not terribly recent. But luckily, one of my old friends still works in the business. I used her as a reference, and she sang my praises to the woman I'll be working for."

"That's terrific, Mom. They're lucky to have you," said Sam. "Everybody always admired our house and you decorated that all by yourself. And I know this house will be equally beautiful."

"And look how beautiful my room is in our little cottage," cried Hannah who had come out on the porch and overheard the discussion. "It's like you knew me, but we'd never met."

"That's a lovely compliment, Hannah. It gave me great pleasure to create a special place for you. I'm glad it feels so personal. That's what I tried for. Anyway, I start next week. I've already talked to Em, and she has agreed to recommend me to any of her clients who are looking for some decorating help. Hopefully I will bring in some business to the firm. And best of all, I only have to be in the office three days a week—the rest of the time I can make my own schedule and do a lot of my work from home. That way, I won't have to be away from you guys too much."

"That's great! I'm really proud of you Mom," said Sam. "It must have been a little scary to go on a job interview after all these years. But leave it to you to get the first job you tried for."

"I'm just lucky, that's all. Now, I want to hear all about your first day at school. Come on; let's go have some of those cookies—if there are any left!"

Rachel put an arm around each of her children and Sam grabbed Hannah's hand as the group trouped up the stairs into the house.

"Andy's teacher is really cool..."

28

The next weekend Rachel and the twins drove to New Jersey to pack up their house. Rachel had listed the house with a realtor friend who felt sure of a quick sale. They spent two days packing clothes, books and kitchen equipment, and Rachel arranged for a mover to transport all the boxes and the furniture that she would be keeping to the Vineyard.

Monday was Martin Luther King Day, a school holiday, so they didn't have to rush back on Sunday. On Monday morning, after they loaded suitcases stuffed with winter clothes into the car, the twins went for a short walk around their old neighborhood, occasionally running into a friend. Rachel stayed at the house, walking slowly from room to room. Each space held memories for her, and she allowed herself the luxury of recalling them; some brought tears but many more, smiles. It had been a wonderful life she and Ben had shared in this house. "But now, I've got to move on," Rachel said aloud to the walls. From the living room window, she watched the twins returning. With a deep breath, she squared her shoulders and stepped out onto the porch, closing the door behind her.

"Come on, guys. We've got a boat to catch!"

• • •

Over the next few weeks, a daily routine for Sam and Andy, as well as Rachel, began to take shape. Two days a week, Sam and Andy rode the school bus to and from school. The other three days, Rachel would drop off the kids at school on her way to her Edgartown office, and the twins would ride the school bus home.

Rachel turned the small entry hall rooms into an office and a meeting space. When she wasn't at the office, she met with clients at home. The work continued on the house, and slowly but surely, it began to reflect the personalities of its new owners. From time to time Rachel sent photographs to Millie Harrington and was gratified by Millie's enthusiastic response to the changes in her old home.

For their parts, Sam and Andy quickly made friends and became involved in several school activities. They also spent a great deal of time with Hannah— especially on weekends when the trio devised adventures of all sorts. Hannah knew the island well and she happily introduced the twins to the uniquely different world of Martha's Vineyard in winter. Scarcely a Saturday passed that the three were not exploring the island from Peaked Hill to Cedar Tree Neck.

Invariably, the conversation would turn to treasure hunts and pirate booty. The three intrepid explorers formed *The Jolly Roger Club*. They had weekly meetings in the tower which they turned into a clubhouse of sorts. It was a tight squeeze for the three of them, but they loved it. They had a battery operated lantern, and they made a table of the old wooden chest that had once held the mysterious diary and map. Sam made everyone an eye patch, and they bought bandanas at Shirley's Hardware store. Rachel found them some old clip on hoop earrings at the thrift shop, and Andy made them cardboard cutlasses. The meetings generally centered on discussions of their future wealth. Millie Harrington had given the enterprise her blessing, so their imaginations knew no limits!

By the mid-February school break, Sam, Andy and Hannah had become an inseparable trio. It was Monday morning, the first day of the vacation, when the phone rang, and Rachel heard a male voice on the other end ask for either Sam or Andy Bennett.

"Sam—Andy—" Rachel called, "phone."

"Who is it?" asked Andy as he thundered down the stairs with Sam close behind.

"May I tell them who's calling?" inquired Rachel.

"Sure, it's Mike Farnsworth from the Historical Society."

"Oh, hi. This is Rachel."

"I thought it might be."

"It's Mike Farnsworth from the Historical Society," whispered Rachel to Sam and Andy excitedly.

"Hello? Hello?" cried Andy, grabbing the phone from Rachel. "This is Andy. Is it real? Is it? Is it?"

Rachel and Sam could hear Mike laughing on the other end of the line.

"Whoa! Slow down. I have some information for you, but I'd like to meet with you in person. Could you by any chance come over to the museum this afternoon?"

"Mom, can we go to the museum this afternoon? Please!!!" begged Andy.

"I'm sure we can manage that. Find out what time would work for Mr. Farnsworth."

"What time would be good?"

"How about two o'clock?"

"Two?" Andy asked Rachel.

"That would be perfect. I'll do the shopping while you two meet with Mr. Farnsworth."

"We can come," shouted Andy.

"Well, good," responded Mike. "I'll see you and Sam at two."

"Cool!" shouted Andy, and they could hear Mike laughing as the call was disconnected.

By the time they left for Edgartown some hours later, Rachel was afraid that Andy was going to have a heart attack. She had been unable to get him to calm down, despite her and Sam's best efforts. Andy had refused lunch and couldn't sit at the table with the rest of them. It was all she could do to get Andy to sit in the car with his seatbelt on for the short drive to the museum.

When they arrived, Andy leapt from the car and ran down the path to the museum entrance. As he burst through the door, the volunteer at the reception desk jumped up in fear and grabbed her purse in order to fend off whatever danger had just invaded her space.

"Where's Mike Farnsworth?" gasped Andy. "I have an appointment."

"Oh," breathed the woman in relief. "He's in the library next door."

"How do I get there?"

"You go back outside with your mother and sister and follow them," said Rachel who stood in the door with a look that Andy and Sam had only seen on a very few unpleasant occasions. "I apologize for my son's inexcusable behavior," said Rachel. "He's a bit over excited."

"I'll say," laughed the woman. "Maybe I should warn Mike."

"Trust me, he will calm down before he gets anywhere near Mike. I hope he didn't frighten you."

"Well, only a little. He certainly does seem intent on his appointment."

"Yes, doesn't he?" responded Rachel in a tone of voice that acted just like a bucket of cold water on Andy's enthusiasm. "Come along, young man," she ordered, and then added sternly, "we're going to have a little talk before you meet Mr. Farnsworth."

With that, they retreated outside and closed the door behind them. Sam was not sure where to look, so she concentrated on her shoes. She knew, as did Andy, that Rachel was angry, and she didn't want to do anything to make things worse, but she had a terrible urge to laugh. Andy looked like some sort of mad scientist—his hair on end, his cheeks flushed, and a sort of glazed look in his eyes.

"Andrew Bennett..." began Rachel.

"Don't say it, Mom. I know. I've been acting like a jerk. I just got so excited. I really want to know what—if—you know—"

"Yes, I do. But that does not excuse your behavior. Now, I want you to go back in there and apologize to that poor woman. Then, we are going to walk calmly over to the library and find Mr. Farnsworth—where your sister will do all and I mean *all* the talking. Is that clear?"

"Yes," whispered a subdued and contrite Andy.

• • •

"All right now, I have good news and bad news," proclaimed Mike

Farnsworth after Sam and Andy had taken the seats he offered them at a large wooden table. "The good news is that the diary is probably authentic, although it still has to be carefully examined by my guy in Boston."

"Wow! That's great!" exclaimed Sam. "What can you tell us about it?"

"It was apparently kept by a young woman named Abigail Cooke."

"Cooke?" questioned Sam, "but the initials on the trunk were A.P."

"Well now, if I recall correctly, Millie Harrington's grandmother was a Prentiss. The Prentiss family lived on Chappy and I'm guessing Abigail Cooke married a Prentiss. The trunk might have been Abigail's hope chest," replied Mike.

"What's a hope chest?" asked Andy.

"I'll explain later," promised Sam.

"So the diary would have been kept by a relative of Millie's?" suggested Rachel.

"Very likely."

"Now the interesting thing is, in the diary Abigail does relate a story her father told her of pirates on the beach near her home, but the geography doesn't match up with the map at all. Also, the paper the map is drawn on is quite old, but—"

"But what?" cried Andy.

"Andrew!" warned Rachel.

"But what?" repeated Andy in a quiet voice.

"But, unfortunately the ink is not old. Although it was made from natural substances like coal soot, my guy in Boston said he doesn't think it's from the same period as the diary and definitely not two hundred years old."

"So, no pirate treasure?" asked Sam

"Not necessarily. It's possible—*possible*," emphasized Mike as Andy appeared likely to launch from his seat, "that the map was redrawn from the original. If the original was falling apart, someone might have made a copy at some later date."

"So, it could really be a map of where the treasure is buried?" asked Sam.

"It could be, yes," replied Mike.

"Wow!" the twins breathed in unison.

"And Mom said you knew where this treasure is supposed to be buried," said Sam.

"I do. And I'll be glad to put you in touch with Mr. Le Grange who owns the property. You aren't the first people to want to try to find the treasure, but I've never heard of anybody with a map before."

"When can we meet him?" asked Andy.

"Not for a while I'm afraid. Tom Le Grange goes to Florida for the winter. He won't be back on the island till late May."

"Well, that would be okay," said Sam. "We won't be finished school till the end of June, but then we'll have all summer."

"All right then, June it is. Give me a call when you're ready and I'll set up a meeting for you with Tom."

"That's awfully kind of you, Mike," said Rachel, "and I know the kids appreciate all that you've done for them. Will you send the kids an invoice for the authentication fee?"

"Sure. You might want to join the Historical Society. We have a family membership that will entitle you to participate in all sorts of interesting activities."

"That sounds good to me. I'll stop at the office on our way out. Thanks again. We'll be in touch in June," said Rachel, extending her hand in farewell.

"I'll look forward to hearing from you," said Mike as he tousled Andy's hair. "See ya, pardner."

"Yeah—see ya," grinned Andy as he bounded out the door with Sam.

"They're terrific. You must be very proud of them," said Mike as Rachel looked after the departing children.

"Oh, I am. They've been remarkable through this whole ordeal. I don't think I would have made it through without them. Well, thanks again for all your help."

"My pleasure."

• • •

In April, Rachel took Sam and Andy to Florida for their spring break to celebrate their birthday with Gommy and Gompy. After a week of sun and swimming, a difficult farewell was made easier with the promise that Gommy and Gompy would come to the Vineyard during the summer for a long visit.

Home again, winter turned to spring, and as the weather warmed, weekends were filled with more long walks all over the island. Never absent from their memory was the trauma of September 11th, but ever so slowly, scar tissue began to form over the pain of their loss and the three survivors began to build a new, if different, life together. As Rachel said to Dan one morning, "I never thought I would ever again be able to refer to my life as normal, but in a strange way, this does seem normal—just a different normal."

"I know what you mean. After Jenny died, nothing felt normal. I guess that's why I started drinking. But thanks to you, I think I'm beginning to feel some kind of normal myself. I don't know how to thank you for giving me—us—this chance," said Dan.

"It's what my Ben would have done. He always believed the best of people. He claimed he'd never been disappointed when he put his faith in people."

"That's not always so easy to do."

"True, but the best things in life are often the most difficult."

29

"Children, may I have your attention for a minute," requested Mrs. McDonough as Sam and her classmates settled into their seats at the first bell. "I have some news. We're going to be getting a new student."

"But school is almost over. How come he's starting now?" asked Katie Clark.

"*She* is starting now so that she can make some new friends before the summer vacation begins."

"A girl!" moaned Peter Strong.

"Yes, a girl," laughed Mrs. McDonough. "She'll be here in a few minutes."

"Actually, she's here right now, Mrs. Mac D," said Principal Binzen from the door. He came into the room followed by a small girl with large brown eyes and a few dark curls that showed under a head scarf.

"This is Hadia Durani," announced Mr. Binzen. "She has only recently arrived from her home in Afghanistan. She is staying with a host family here on the Vineyard. I know you will make her feel welcome and help her learn her way around. Hadia, we are very glad you have come and we hope you will be happy here on the Vineyard."

"Thank you very much," replied the little girl in accented but perfect English.

"Your English is excellent, Hadia," said Mrs. Mc Donough.

"Thank you. My father was a professor at the university in Kabul before the Taliban. He taught me English."

"He did a fine job. Now let's see, where should you sit? Sam and Lucy, would you mind separating your desks so Hadia could sit between you? That way she will have two guides to help her find her way!"

"Sure," agreed Lucy. Sam nodded in agreement, and the girls began to move their desks.

"Sam is also fairly new to our school, Hadia, so she knows what you're experiencing. Lucy has lived on the Vineyard all her life, so she'll be able to help you find your way round town."

"Thank you so much," said Hadia gratefully. "You are all so kind. You make me feel very welcome."

"And you <u>are</u>, Hadia. We are all very glad you are here—aren't we class?"

• • •

Sam immediately took Hadia under her wing and asked her to join her and the other girls at a table in the lunch room. It was hard not to notice the stares and whispering as the students in other classes noticed Hadia for the first time.

"Don't worry," said Sam. "They're just curious. Why do Muslim women wear a head scarf?"

"It is a sign of modesty. In some places in Afghanistan, the women have to wear a chadri. That is a garment which covers a woman completely except for a small opening around the eyes covered in netting."

"Why?" asked Lucy.

"The Taliban says that women are unclean and a temptation to men, so they must be covered when they are out in public. In Afghanistan, under the Taliban, a woman could not walk in public unless she was with a man who was a relative. She was not allowed to make eye contact with a man other than her husband."

"But I thought the Taliban were overthrown when the American soldiers came to Afghanistan," said Annie.

"It is true that the Taliban have lost some of their power, but there are places where they still have great influence. My uncle is sure they will try to regain control. And in my village, the Taliban are still very powerful. If the Taliban regain control, those who have sided with the Americans will be in great danger."

• • •

"How was school today?" asked Rachel as she ladled clam chowder into bowls that night at dinner.

"Boring!" cried Andy, laughing, as he reached for the basket of hot rolls.

"Oh you! You always say that. I think you just like to torture your old mother," accused Rachel.

"Not true—but come on Mom—the last few days of school are always boring."

"Well, it wasn't boring in my room," said Sam helping herself to salad. "We got a new student."

"Really? It's awfully late to be starting school. There are only two weeks left," said Rachel.

"Yeah, I know," replied Sam, "but her host family wanted her to have a chance to meet some kids before the vacation."

"Her 'host' family?" repeated Andy, with raised eyebrows.

"Yes. Her name is Hadia and she just came from Afghanistan," reported Sam.

"Wow—that's very interesting. How did she end up here from Afghanistan? Seems like an odd place to come to," said Rachel.

"I'm not sure," answered Sam. "I know her father is a professor at the university in Kabul. Her uncle thought she would be safer in America. Her mother and brother are still in Afghanistan. She seems really nice."

"Right," mumbled Andy under his breath.

"What honey?" asked Rachel.

"Nothing—may I be excused please?"

"What? You haven't touched your dinner. Eat your soup. It's your favorite—clam chowder from The Clam Shack."

"Not hungry."

Andy shoved himself away from the table and ran out of the dining room. Sam and Rachel exchanged confused looks as Andy stomped up the stairs and slammed his bedroom door.

"I guess I'll give him a little time to calm down. Let's finish our supper anyway."

"Okay, Mom," said Sam. Her concern about her brother's behavior had dampened her enthusiasm for the good supper her mother had prepared and the two finished quickly, in silence.

"Do you mind washing up for me?" asked Rachel when they were finished. "I'd like to take some supper up to Andy and see if I can get to the bottom of this."

"No problem, Mom. Want me to nuke his chowder?"

"That would be great. I'll put a tray together."

A few minutes later Rachel, carrying a tray, tapped gently but firmly on Andy's door.

"What?" came the gruff response.

"It's Mom. Can I come in?"

"I guess so."

Rachel opened the door and went in, closing the door behind her. Andy was seated on the bench under his window, looking out at the water. In his lap was a framed photo of Andy and Ben on a fishing expedition when Andy had caught a tremendous bluefish. As the door clicked shut, Andy looked up at his mother and Rachel could see that his face was tearstained.

"That was quite a fishing trip—wasn't it?" she smiled.

"Yeah," was the one word reply.

"You want to talk about it?"

"What—the fishing trip?"

"No—whatever it was that caused you to leave the dinner table like you were riding an ejector seat."

"My sister. How can Sam—she—I don't get it"

"Don't get what?"

"She's a terrorist!" he shouted.

"Sam is a terrorist? What on earth are you talking about?" exclaimed Rachel, her mouth open in shock at such an outlandish remark.

"Not Sam, Mom. That girl—whatever her name is—that new girl. She's a terrorist. How can Sam say she's nice?"

"Her name is Hadia, if I recall correctly, and she is not a terrorist. She's a child just like you."

"No, she's not just like me. She's from Afghanistan. They flew the planes into the World Trade Center and the Pentagon. They're all terrorists!" he shouted.

Despite the closed door, Sam heard Andy shout and nearly dropped the bowl she was rinsing in her shock over such a remark. It seemed totally out of character for Andy. She knew it wasn't right, but Sam ignored her normally high moral standards, dried the bowl she had been washing, and quietly climbed the stairs. She knelt outside Andy's door and listened intently.

"Andrew Jason Bennett! As far as I know, none of the men who flew those planes were from Afghanistan.

"Yeah, but Osama Bin Laden is hiding there. They're protecting him. They're just as bad. They're all the same."

"We've talked about this. You can't generalize about people."

"Yeah, well, I've changed my opinion," snapped Andy.

"Since when?"

"Since one of them came to my town, to my school."

"Andy, you haven't even met this girl. What does it say about you that you would judge her so harshly simply because of where she was born?"

"Because she was born in a country full of people that want to kill us!"

"Andy, you know better," said Sam quietly from the door. "Remember when we learned about discrimination at Williams Street? We learned how people stereotyped the different immigrant groups that came to America? You and I talked about how awful it was, and we agreed we would never think that way about people."

"I never had a reason to before."

"What changed?"

"Are you for real? What changed? What changed was they murdered our father!" he screamed.

"Who is 'they'?" asked Rachel.

"The men who flew those planes!" snapped Andy as if his mother was some sort of moron.

"Andy, I repeat. The men who flew those planes were not from Afghanistan."

"So? They were trained in Afghanistan. And they were Muslims. They're all the same."

"So all Muslims are terrorists?"

"Yes!"

"Andy—remember Oklahoma City?" asked Sam.

"Of course."

"The men who did that were terrorists. They were also Americans. Does that mean all Americans are terrorists?"

"No—but—"

"But what? You can't have one set of rules for Americans and another set for the rest of the world!" cried Sam. "And while we're on this subject, what do you think Dad would say if he could hear you talking like this?"

To that, Andy had no response.

30

"Mrs. McDonough, could we have an Open Circle?"

"I think we could. Everyone bring your chairs to circle please."

The children picked up their chairs and moved them to an open space in the back of the room, placing them in a circle. Hadia followed their lead, positioning her chair next to Sam's. Mrs. Mc Donough sat on the other side of Hadia.

"Hadia, Open Circle is an idea that Sam brought to our class from her other school in New Jersey. We use it as a way to discuss issues and problems that the class is trying to deal with. Sam, since you asked for the circle, I assume you have something you would like to talk about."

"My—" Sam hesitated and then started again. "Someone I know is really prejudiced against a particular group of people, and I have a friend who's a member of this group."

"Do you know why the person feels this way?" inquired Lucy.

"Yes, and I understand it, but it's still wrong to generalize about a whole group. I don't know what I can do to help change his mind."

"Does your friend actually know anyone who is part of the group?" asked Henry.

"Not that I know of."

"Perhaps," suggested Hadia quietly, "if you could arrange for that to happen, your friend would realize the error of his thinking."

"I'm not sure how to do that. It would be pretty obvious that the person is a member of this group."

"Why? Is your friend prejudiced against black people or something?" asked Louis, a young African-American classmate.

"No—" Sam hesitated.

"Is it the way the person dresses, then, that would give it away?" asked Hadia.

Sam nodded silently, afraid to meet Hadia's gaze.

"Perhaps if I removed my headscarf, your friend would not know," suggested Hadia as she took Sam's hand. Sam looked into the dark brown eyes, so full of understanding, so full of pain.

The bell rang.

• • •

"Why didn't you stay in Afghanistan?" asked Lucy later at lunch.

"I wish I could have. But after my father was killed by the Taliban, my uncle thought it would be better for me here."

"That's horrible!" cried Sam. "Why did they kill your father?"

"Because he was not a fanatic, like the Taliban. His religion was very important to him, but it was not the only thing. For example, he thought women should be allowed to go to school and have jobs just like men, but the Taliban believe that women who are educated are unholy. That is not what most Muslims think. My Uncle knew that if I stayed in Afghanistan, I might never have a chance at an education. And he was worried that I would be a target for the Taliban as my father had been, so he sent me to America."

"I wish my, uh, friend could hear your story," said Sam.

"Sam, believe me when I tell you that I understand how people feel about me and my country. I know that trust has to be earned."

"But Hadia—if Sam trusts you, everyone should," asserted Anne.

"I do not understand, Anne. Why is Sam different from anyone else?" asked Hadia. Anne did not see the warning look Sam shot at her across the table.

"Because of her father," said Anne innocently.

"Sam?" questioned Hadia. "What is it about your father that I should know?"

"That you killed him," growled a voice behind Hadia. She whipped around and looked up into a face that was filled with anger—perhaps hatred. Andy flicked at Hadia's headscarf.

"You're in America—dress like an American."

"Andy—stop it! What is wrong with you? Leave her alone!" cried Sam.

"What's wrong with *me*? What's wrong with *you*? She murdered your father!"

"No, Andy," said Sam. "The men who flew those planes murdered my father, not this girl, not her family or her friends—the men who flew the planes. Now get lost!"

"You're all crazy!" retorted Andy as he walked away in disgust.

Hadia stared at Sam with such a look of horror on her face that Sam could barely meet her gaze.

"Sam—Sam, it cannot be —your father . . ." she trailed off.

"Yes. He was in the North Tower of the World Trade Center on nine-eleven," said Sam quietly.

"I am without words. And that, I assume, was your friend who hates all Muslims?"

"A friend? No—worse. Much worse." Hadia looked questioningly at Sam. "He's my brother."

Hadia reached across the table and took Sam's hand.

Just then the bell rang. As the girls were returning their trays, Andy passed by. He put his tray down, turned and left without speaking to Sam or even acknowledging her presence.

"Try not to let a few idiots like my brother make you think badly about all Americans."

"I will not. I am so grateful to have friends like you and Lucy and Katie and Annie and all the other nice people I have met. Sam, I understand how Andy feels. I might feel the same way about a child of a Taliban official. Perhaps someday Andy will change his mind about me, but in the meanwhile, I will try to be a good friend to you!"

The serious little group left the cafeteria to return to their classrooms.

• • •

"Mrs. McD, do you think Hadia could tell us about her country?" asked Sam.

"Oh, Sam, I think that would be a wonderful idea. This last week of school is always so fractured. I think it would be a wonderful way to end the year. Would you be willing to do that, Hadia?"

"Yes, if the other students would be interested."

"I would be," said Lucy quietly.

"Me, too," added Katie. One by one the other students agreed that they would like to learn more about Afghanistan.

"Well, why don't those of you who are interested make a list of questions that you have about Afghanistan? May we include Islam as well, Hadia?"

"Oh yes. I would be most happy to explain about my faith."

"Excellent. Why don't you put something together, and let me know when you're ready. Any day next week would be fine."

"Of course. And thank you," replied Hadia.

"Mrs. McDonough, could we invite Mr. Hazlet's class?" asked Sam.

"I think that would be a wonderful idea. I'll speak to him after school."

The rest of the afternoon passed quickly, and it was almost a surprise when the bell rang for dismissal.

"I can't wait to hear about your country," said Katie. "My mom has a friend who lived in Iran for a while, but that was when the Shah was still in power. She has told me a lot about Iran when she lived there. Is Afghanistan like Iran?"

"Not really. They are similar geographically because they both have great mountains but, we don't have as many big cities as Iran. We are more simple. I don't know the word—like—farm land."

"Rural?" suggested Sam.

"Yes, rural. That is the word. Thank you. My English vocabulary is not as good as it should be."

"Well, it's a lot better than my Afghan vocabulary!" laughed Sam.

"Sam, would you—perhaps I should not ask you of all people, but you have been so kind. Would you help me to prepare my talk about Afghanistan?"

"I would be happy to, Hadia. Maybe we can get together after school tomorrow and I can help you collect some materials to use."

"That would be wonderful. Thank you."

• • •

"So how was school today?" asked Rachel as she sat down to dinner with the twins.

"Oh peachy," replied Andy, "for Sam and her new best friend."

"Andy was rude and cruel to her in public. He made fun of her for wearing a headscarf—and he hasn't even been introduced to her. He behaved horribly. Daddy would have been furious."

"Andy, is this true?"

"No. I treated her the way she deserved. Her and all the rest of them."

"Them? Who is 'them'?"

"You know—"

"*Muslims?*"

"They killed Dad."

"Andy, we talked about this. You cannot hold all Muslims accountable for what a small group of fanatics did.

"And I agree with Sam. Your father would not be proud of your behavior, nor would he agree with your feelings. So if you want to honor your father, I would try to keep an open mind about this young girl. She had nothing whatever to do with nine-eleven and she is probably having a pretty scary experience being sent here to America.

"You know, if you don't like the way Muslim's think about America, you have a great opportunity to change that, at least in a small way, by showing Hadia that Americans don't judge people based on their religion or their nationality. What was it Martin Luther King said? '...not by the color of their skin, but by the content of their character.'"

"And let's just hope Hadia doesn't think your behavior today is a sign of your character. I certainly hope not," said Sam.

Chastened, Andy asked quietly, "May I please be excused?"

"Yes, I think that would be a good idea," said Rachel. "Why don't you spend some time in your room thinking about what I've just said?"

31

adia's voice shook a little as she began. "First, I would like to thank Mrs. McDonough for this opportunity to tell you about Afghanistan. Also, I must thank Sam who has helped me to find materials for my talk. She has drawn some beautiful maps and pictures. In case you did not know, Sam is a wonderful artist."

"She is?" snorted Andy, whose class had been invited to hear Hadia's presentation. "Could have fooled me."

Tension had run high since Andy and his class had entered Mrs. McDonough's room. It increased when Mrs. McDonough had called the two girls to the front of the room.

Both girls ignored the comment and Hadia continued.

"Afghanistan is a very poor country. Most of the people live on less than two dollars US a day. We have a few big cities, but most of our land is used for farming and much of it is mountainous. We have been invaded and occupied many times in our history, most recently by the Soviet Union and now, of course, by the United States."

"We came to help you!" shouted Andy.

"I know, Andy," agreed Hadia quietly.

She glanced at Sam who nodded encouragement. Sam had an awful feeling that nothing her mother had said to Andy had sunk in.

"Andy," Hadia continued, "think for a minute what it would be like to have foreign soldiers in your country.

"In America, you have never known occupation or had to fight a foreign army on your own land since your Revolution. Can you imagine how terrifying it is to have bombs being dropped on your village or gun battles raging in your streets? Believe me, it doesn't matter if the bullet that killed your brother or your mother came from the gun of a friend or an enemy. They are still dead." Andy did not reply, but began doodling furiously on a piece of paper as Hadia continued.

"Afghanistan is made up of many different groups of people. Most are members of a tribe or a clan. They are very proud and protection of the clan comes first—even before protection of the country. We speak over a dozen different languages, although Pashtun and Tariq are the most common. We are a Muslim country as are many Middle Eastern countries. And like many religions, there are those who believe that all other faiths are wrong and— Sam what is that word I can never pronounce?"

"Blasphemous?"

"Yes, blasphemous. But most believe that everyone is entitled to their own beliefs. You know, even though there has been a lot of fighting and killing between religions, many things are the same in the Christian, Jewish and Muslim faiths. Some parts of our holy books are the same. We believe that many of the same places are holy; like Jerusalem. We share many of the same prophets. We may have different names for God, but all three religions believe in one God. I myself do not understand why it is so hard for us to live in peace."

"Because you people keep trying to kill us!" said Andy quietly.

"Andy, if you cannot control yourself, you will have to leave the room," cautioned Mrs. McDonough.

"Fine," said Andy and headed for the classroom door.

"Andy," said Mrs. Mac Donough quietly, "if you leave, you will be doing exactly what the terrorists want."

"Right!" scoffed Andy. "How do you figure?"

"Because the reason we cannot live in peace is because we do not understand who the *others* are. Somehow we have gotten the idea that to respect another's religion means we must believe in it. Many people seem to think that if someone else's religion or culture is allowed to exist, then theirs cannot," said Mrs. Mc Donough.

"Andy, my father believed that education was the key to peace in the world," Hadia said softly, "because we are afraid of things we don't understand. He said education helps us understand about other ideas, other people. But, Andy, we will never understand until we listen. I am not asking you to agree with what I say. I only ask you to listen. Then, see how you feel. Make your choices from knowledge, not from fear."

"Come on, Andy," called one of the boys, "you're always talking about being a proud American. Well, Americans believe in listening to all sides. The least you can do is listen."

"Yeah!" cried another voice and more joined in. Slowly, Andy returned to his seat, and although he would not look at Hadia for the remainder of her talk, from time to time other students noticed his looks of surprise or interest in some of the things Hadia had to say.

A half hour later, Hadia drew her talk to a close.

"I hope you have found my presentation interesting. And now I have brought a little treat for you. These are a traditional Afghani pastry called *Asabia el Aroos* or *Brides Fingers*. They are similar to Baklava only not quite as sweet or sticky. I hope you will try them. I am not such a good cook as my mother, but Sam tried one and as you can see, she is still breathing, so I think they are safe!"

The class laughed—even Andy, although he tried to hide it.

"Does anyone have any questions for Hadia?" asked Mrs. Mc Donough as the girls passed around the trays laden with the tempting pastries.

"I know your father was killed, Hadia, but where is your mother?" asked Lucy.

"She is still in Afghanistan. I have a little brother. My mother and brother live with my Uncle—my mother's brother—and his family."

Andy raised his hand. Hadia tried to hide the surprise she felt. "Yes, Andy?"

"Why didn't they come to the states?" he asked.

"You may find this hard to understand, given what I have told you about the poverty and the difficulty of life in Afghanistan, but we love our country. We know it isn't perfect, but it is our country.

"Also, my mother, like many Afghani women, is not educated and she would have no way of making a living here. She also wants my brother to have a traditional Muslim education. Not—" she said quickly as Andy's face clouded over, "a fanatic's version, but a true Islamic education which includes studying our religion and its teachings as well as all the regular subjects.

"I was sent here because my father wanted me to go to university, but as of now, that is not possible for a girl in Afghanistan, although I hope that by the time I am ready it might be. In the meanwhile, I will study hard, learning about people and ideas, as my father would have wanted."

"Don't you miss them?" he asked quietly.

"Of course—wouldn't you miss your family if they were not here?"

"I do," whispered Andy quietly.

There was a long pause before Hadia spoke.

"Andy, I hope you will believe me when I tell you how sorry I am that your father was a victim of the terrible men who attacked the World Trade Center. I am even sorrier that those men were Muslims. I am ashamed of what they did. And I believe that most Muslim people feel that way, too. But I also want you to know that I and many people in Afghanistan are grateful for the help they are receiving from the United States. I will pray to God every night that He will keep all the American soldiers safe from harm and that your dear father and mine will share in God's heaven together."

"Your God or mine?" asked Andy, choking back tears.

"I believe they are the same, Andy; one and the same."

32

"I'm almost afraid to ask. How did it go today?"

There was silence in the room.

"Andy?"

"It was—okay—I guess."

"How was Hadia's presentation?"

"Sam made some cool maps and stuff."

"*How was Hadia's presentation?*"

"It was—really interesting," admitted Andy with a sheepish smile. "I'm sorry, Mom. I guess I was being a real jerk."

"Well, I really do understand where your feelings were coming from, Andy. But what did Hadia say that changed your mind?"

"She talked about the need to listen to other people's ideas and to try to respect their ideas even if you don't agree with them."

"And how did that help?"

"Because-" Andy choked back tears, "because it sounded so much like something Dad would say. I could hear his voice in my head, and he was telling me—telling me—"

"What?" asked Sam quietly, speaking for the first time since they had sat down.

Tears coursed down Andy's face. "Telling me he was ash—ashamed of me," he hiccupped.

Rachel knelt by Andy's chair. "Your father would never be ashamed of you. He would understand that you were being ruled by your emotions. He would be so proud of you for being able to get past all that anger and hurt and really listen to what Hadia had to say."

"I agree," said Sam. "And I was proud of you, too, A."

"Honest—I don't think anyone should be proud of me. No matter what I do, I can't take back what I did to Hadia. She'll never forgive me."

"You know, I don't know Hadia all that well—but she doesn't strike me as the type to hold a grudge. I'll bet if you apologize to her, she'll forgive you," predicted Sam.

"I guess it couldn't get any worse. I'll give it a try."

• • •

And the next day at the class picnic at State Beach, Andy did just that.

Hadia was seated with Sam and several other girls under a beach umbrella sharing the picnic lunches they had brought with them. The girls, except for Hadia, were all wearing bathing suits or shorts. Hadia wore gauzy cotton pants with a tunic that came to below her knees and a head scarf, all in a lovely swirling blue and green pattern that reminded Sam of the sea.

"So you could wear a bathing suit as long as there weren't any boys around?"

"Yes. Muslims consider it immodest for a woman to swim with men or boys."

"Is it okay to talk to them?" asked Andy as he joined the circle of friends.

Hadia looked up and smiled at Andy. "Of course, Andy. Shall we walk?"

"Yes, please," exhaled Andy, relieved that he would not have to say his apology in front of Sam and her other friends. The two young people excused themselves and walked along the shoreline, splashing through the water as they walked.

They were silent for a few minutes, and then Andy got his courage up to speak.

"Hadia, I want to apologize for all the terrible things I said and for trying to pull off your—hijab. Is that how you say it?"

"Yes, that is just right Andy. And I forgive you. I understand so well how you must have felt. I'm sure I might have similar feelings if I were in school with a child of a Taliban leader."

"I don't know how you can be so—so — well, I wouldn't forgive me if I were you."

"Andy, I am going to live here for the next several years. Sam is my first friend. I like her very much, and we have much in common. You are her brother whom she loves very dearly. I know that because Sam loves you, you must be a wonderful person. I would like to have a wonderful person for another of my friends. And I never want Sam to feel she has to choose between the two of us."

"Well, I guess the same goes for me. I never thought about it that way. If I had, I would have realized that Sam would never have been friends with someone who wasn't a good person. Boy, I guess I've been dumb in more ways than one. You sure you want to be friends with me?"

"Andy, it is hard to admit a mistake, but you have. Now let us not make another by missing the ice cream which is being served under the tent over there. Come on!" cried Hadia as she began to run along the beach toward the white tent that had been set up to shelter the refreshments from the sun.

"Wait up," laughed Andy as he took off after Hadia.

Hadia turned, jogging in place until Andy caught up with her. "Boy, you run fast—for a girl!"

"I have many talents!" she laughed.

33

And so began what was to be a lasting and true friendship between Andy, Sam, Hannah and Hadia. The first order of business was to officially welcome Hadia to *The Jolly Roger Club*. The meeting was moved to the porch as it was too hot in the tower.

"The meeting of The Jolly Roger Club is called to order!" announced Sam, who had been chosen Captain of the Ship. "I make a motion that Hadia come aboard as a shipmate of The Jolly Roger Club."

"I second the motion!" cried Hannah.

"All in favor?"

"Aye!" chorused three voices enthusiastically.

"Thank you—I accept!" laughed Hadia.

"Now that you're a shipmate, we can tell you about the pirate treasure," declared Andy who smiled at the surprised look on Hadia's face.

A half hour later, the story had been shared and many opinions expressed about the truth of the tale and the possibility of finding the treasure. A group decision was made that Andy should call Mike Farnsworth and try to arrange a meeting with Tom Le Grange on Chappaquiddick.

"I'm going to go call him right now," said Andy as he hurried into the house.

Not long after, he was back. "Mike said he would call Mr. Le Grange tomorrow and would let us know. He said he thought Mr. Le Grange was going off island for a couple of days, so it might be next week before we can meet with him."

"Well, that's disappointing," sighed Sam.

"Since we can't do anything today, let's go on a picnic!" cried Hannah.

"And how about an overnight tonight?" suggested Sam. "Hadia, do you think you can stay over?"

"I will call Mrs. Dressler, but I don't see why not."

An hour later, full of sandwiches, potato chips, iced tea and chocolate chip cookies, the quartet was relaxing in the warm sun when Sam asked Hadia, "Would you ever marry someone who wasn't a Muslim?"

"I couldn't say positively 'no,'" replied Hadia, "but it seems not likely. First of all, my Mother and Uncle would probably never agree to it and I would not go against them. My faith is very important to me. It would be very difficult to be a good Muslim wife married to a Christian or a Jew. Would you marry a Muslim?"

"I don't think so," Sam admitted honestly. "I don't think Mom would mind—if I really loved him. I don't think I could be a good Muslim wife, though, and I probably wouldn't be very happy."

"Well, I guess that means we'll all just have to be friends!" exclaimed Andy. "How about a game of Frisbee?"

"Yes, please!" cried Hannah.

The rest of the afternoon passed pleasantly and after a supper of barbequed chicken and fresh corn, the happy group spread sleeping bags out on the lawn and stargazed until they fell asleep.

• • •

They were just finishing breakfast the next morning when the phone rang.

"Andy," called Rachel from the living room, "it's Mike Farnsworth for you."

Andy ran to the phone. "Hi, this is Andy. . . .Yes, right. I see. . . . Okay. I think that will be fine. . . . Right—Tuesday at eleven. That's great. Thanks, Mike. Bye."

He ran back to the kitchen table and announced, "Mr. Le Grange says we can come Tuesday at eleven. Mike said to come to the Museum around ten and he'll give us directions."

"Pirate treasure, here we come!" shouted Hannah.

To which the other three replied loudly, "Arrrrrgh!"

34

The following Tuesday morning, a hot and somewhat bedraggled group arrived at the Museum library after their six mile bike ride from Oak Bluffs. Shovels were strapped to the backs of their bikes, pails hung off the handlebars, and backpacks were stuffed with everything from sun screen to bottled water and tuna fish sandwiches.

Sam opened the door to the library and stepped into the bookshelf lined room that held the Museum's reference materials, followed by her fellow buccaneers. The large work tables held a variety of books and pamphlets. Behind the desk sat Mike Farnsworth.

"Hi guys! Right on time. Are you psyched?"

"Oh man, are we ever!" cried Andy.

"All right then. I won't keep you, but who are these two beautiful ladies you've brought with you?" asked Mike gallantly.

"Oh, I'm sorry," apologized Sam. "This is Hannah Furman. Her dad, Dan, is the contractor for the renovations on our house. Hannah and her dad live in our guest house. And this is Hadia Durani. She's from Afghanistan and she just moved here. We were in the same class together this year. They're going to help us dig for the treasure."

"Well, it seems you've assembled a first class team. Mr. Le Grange is expecting you. I'll give him a call when you leave here and let him know you're on your way." Mike went on to give them directions on how to find Mr. Le Grange's house on Chappaquiddick.

"If you're back before six, stop by here, because I think I might have some news for you about the diary by then."

"Wow, that would be great!" exclaimed Andy.

"Okay, now ride safely. There are a lot of cars on Chappy this time of year. And take it easy. It's a pretty long ride and it's hot out there."

"We'll be careful. And thanks, Mike," called Sam as the group departed for the little ferry that would take them across to their own Treasure Island.

The four bicycled through the beautiful seaside village of Edgartown and followed the signs to the Chappaquiddick ferry. Technically, Chappaquiddick is not really an island, because at certain times of the year it is possible to drive to it from the beach on the Atlantic coast of the island, but for much of the year, it is cut off from the mainland. Those who live or visit there depend on the little open ferry, the *On Time*, to carry them across. It is aptly named since there is no published schedule for when the ferry runs, so it is always "on time". On this day there was a long line of cars waiting to cross but only a few cyclists, so it took only two trips before the four adventurers walked their bikes onto the little ferry and set off across the channel.

Once on the other side, they consulted the directions which Mike had provided and set off on their ride to Mr. Le Grange's home.

It was indeed a long ride. As they looked out over the ocean, it was easy to imagine a pirate ship anchoring here and thinking it was a fine place to bury treasure, especially since there had been few people living here in Josiah Cooke's time.

They found Mr. Le Grange's mailbox and headed down a rutted dirt road. Finally, as they rounded a bend in the road, they saw a tidy little house with a flourishing vegetable garden and an old skiff up on saw horses in the yard. An older gentleman, busy scraping peeling paint from the hull of the skiff, looked up as the quartet rode into the yard.

"Well, now, you must be the young treasure hunters Mike Farnsworth called me about."

"Yes, sir," replied Sam nervously. "I'm Sam and this is my brother, Andy. These are our friends Hannah and Hadia."

"You're a fine looking crew, and I hope you'll find a chest of gold doubloons!" he chuckled.

"So do we!" exclaimed Andy.

"Well, I don't want to discourage you, but an awful lot of people have searched in vain for this treasure over the years. Still, it's an interesting tale, and it can't hurt to try again."

"Could you tell us the story," asked Hadia. "Sam and Andy told me a little, but I would love to know the real tale."

"I think I could manage. Why don't we get something cool to drink, and I'll see what I can remember."

A few minutes later, with cold glasses of cranberry juice in hand and a plate of sugar cookies, the group was seated on a ragtag collection of chairs in back of the house as Mr. Le Grange began his tale.

"So, now, pirates is it? Yes, there were some pirates in this part of the world back in the seventeen hundreds. They were called Mooncussers, and mostly they smuggled things."

"Why were they called Mooncussers?" asked Hannah.

"Because they had to get in and out under cover of darkness. When the moonlight was bright, they were more likely to be caught, so they would swear or cuss at the moon."

"Weren't there any real pirates, like Captain Kidd or Blackbeard?" asked Andy.

"Oh, there is definitely a school of thought that believes that both those cutthroats visited our little island. In fact, there are some who think the legend of the blue boulder was really about Blackbeard."

"Cool! So, what is the whole story?" asked Andy.

"The way I've heard it is this. A farmer named Josiah Cooke lived here on Chappy and raised some cattle. One night during a fierce nor'easter, he couldn't find one of his cows and he went out to look for it. Somehow he ended up at the beach where he saw pirates land and drag a big chest up onto the beach near a huge bluestone bolder. Two pirates dug a hole large enough to hold the chest and lowered it into the hole. Then, as the story goes, the Captain shot the two men, pushed them into the hole and buried them along with the treasure."

"Gee, nice guy!" joked Andy

"Cooke returned later to search for the treasure, but all traces of where the treasure had been buried were gone."

"But wait—you said it was near a big blue boulder," objected Sam.

"Ah, you were listening. Good for you, Sam. Indeed, the treasure was buried near a big blue boulder."

"So why couldn't Mr. Cooke find it?" asked Andy.

"Come on with me, and I'll show you," replied Mr. Le Grange mysteriously.

The group gathered their backpacks, shovels and pails and followed Mr. Le Grange along a sandy path and through tall beach grass. Suddenly the whole expanse of shoreline opened up before them, and they stepped onto the white sand beach.

"Of course, I have no way of telling where Cooke actually hid to watch the pirates, but if you look over that way," he said pointing, "you'll see what the problem was."

Four heads turned to where Mr. Le Grange pointed, and all four exclaimed in despair, "Oh, no!" For there, along the beach, was not one, but three blue boulders.

"But which one was it?" asked Hannah.

"Nobody knows," replied Mr. Le Grange. "I'm guessing that Cooke tried digging near them all, but according to the legend, he never found anything. Plenty of people have looked since without success."

"Do you think we are wasting our time?" asked Hadia.

"Depends on what you want."

"What do you mean?" questioned Andy.

"I mean, if you want the fun of *searching* for treasure, then here's an adventure waiting for you. But, if you're only interested in *finding* the treasure, then I might say you should maybe forget about it. The adventure is in the searching, not the finding."

The four looked at each other, and somehow a silent understanding was reached.

"Okay, two on this first rock and two on the second," commanded Andy.

"If we don't find anything, we'll all work on the third," suggested Sam.

"I'll work with Sam," declared Hadia.

"Come on, Andy, let's get digging!" cried Hannah.

As the four took off down the beach toward their rocks, they didn't hear Mr. Le Grange's satisfied laughter.

They dug and dug, excavating the sand around all three boulders, but they did not find what they were searching for. They did find a dollar and twenty-six cents in change, as well as two pairs of broken sunglasses, a pink flip flop, a toy dump truck and an old paperback book. Laughing and cheering with each discovery, they finally collapsed, exhausted, backs against the largest of the three boulders and shared their picnic lunches as the sun began its descent toward the horizon. It was nearly four o'clock, and the light was that wonderful clear blue light that makes everything look sharp and clear.

"I guess we won't be rich," concluded Andy.

"But we sure had fun, didn't we?" asked Sam.

"We did. And who needs money anyway?" challenged Hannah.

"Well..."

"Andy!" scolded the other three.

"Oh, I'm just kidding. But come on, we'd better go thank Mr. Le Grange and head back. It'll take us a while to get home, and Mike said he would only be there till six."

After a brief visit with Mr. Le Grange, who invited them to visit whenever they wanted, the weary explorers pedaled back to the ferry landing and crossed back to Edgartown. They arrived back at the Museum just at six, and Mike was just locking the door of the library.

"Wow—good timing. Another few minutes and you'd have missed me. So did you find the treasure?"

"Nah—but we had fun anyway," answered Andy.

"I'm glad. Tom Le Grange is a terrific guy."

"Yes, we enjoyed meeting him. He told us the whole story of Farmer Cooke and his missing cow," reported Hadia.

"Mike, you said you might have some information for us about the diary," Sam reminded him. "Do you?"

"Actually I do—and I think you're going to like it. My friend to whom I sent the diary called me this afternoon and confirmed that the diary was authentic. He has a client who would like to buy it from you and then donate it to the Museum."

"Cool!" shouted Andy. "How much do we get?"

"Quite a lot, actually — fifteen hundred dollars."

"I think I'm going to faint, Sam. Catch me."

"Too late, brother — I feel a little faint myself. Did you say fifteen hundred dollars?"

"I did. Congratulations. That's a lot of money. What are you going to do with it?"

"I have no idea," whispered Andy, still in a state of shock. "I guess we'll have to think about it."

"Should I tell my friend that you accept his offer?"

"I think we had better discuss it with Mom," said Sam.

"I think you're right. Why don't you have a family conference and let me know what you want to do. If you decide to accept the offer, we can get started on the paperwork."

"Paperwork?"

"Yes. When you sell something like this, you have to have proof that says you actually own it and have the right to sell it."

"Gosh, I guess we better call Millie, then. Would a letter from Millie be enough proof?" asked Sam.

"I think that would be fine," answered Mike.

"Come on, guys. Mike has already stayed an extra half hour for us. Mike can we call you in the morning?" asked Sam.

"You bet. I'll look forward to hearing from you."

"Okay, great. And thanks a million for introducing us to Mr. Le Grange," called Sam as the four rode off toward the bike path that would lead them back to Oak Bluffs.

35

"Pizza's here," called Dan as he came around the corner of the house to the front porch where the children had been regaling Rachel with the details of their visit with Tom Le Grange.

"Thank goodness!" cried Andy, "I'm starving."

"There's news," laughed Sam. "You're always hungry."

"Yeah, yeah. Which one's the pepperoni?"

Quiet settled over the happy group as everyone settled down with pizza and soda to watch the sky darken as the sun set behind them.

"I guess we have to call Millie," said Rachel.

"Yeah, we'll need a letter from her," said Sam.

"I know she gave you permission to pursue this, but when she learns how much money is involved, it might be a different story," suggested Rachel.

"You mean she may want the money?" asked Hannah.

"Yes. Have you guys thought about how you will feel if that happens?" asked Rachel.

"I guess we'll feel sort of bad," said Andy, "but it would also be fair—kind of."

"Yeah, who knows? Maybe Millie needs money. I mean, she doesn't work or anything," added Sam.

"That's true," agreed Rachel, proud of her children for their unselfish thinking.

"And it's not like we need the money. I can't think of anything I want that I don't already have," said Sam.

"I know what you mean," said Hadia. "Sometimes, I feel sort of sorry for myself and wish I could go home and be with my family, but then I think how lucky I am compared to other girls who are still in Afghanistan. I have the Dressler's lovely home to live in, a good school to attend and wonderful friends," she added quietly.

"I think we're all as lucky as can be!" cried Hannah.

"Me, too," agreed Sam, "and no matter what Millie decides, I wouldn't have done anything differently. Besides, she might tell us to go ahead, sell the diary and keep the money. We just have to have—"

"A positive attitude!" cried six happy, laughing voices.

• • •

"Hi,—Mrs. Harrington? This is Andy Bennett from the Vineyard," explained Andy an hour later. "Oh no, Mam, everyone is fine. How are you?"

"She's fine" Andy reported to the group.

"Hi Mrs. H!" called the others.

"She's laughing. She says 'Hi!' back."

"Anyway Mrs. H., the reason I'm calling is—you know the diary we found up in the tower? Okay, so we took it to the museum, and they had it — Mom— what was it they did?"

"They authenticated it."

"Right. They authenticated it. Well, they authenticated the diary anyway, not the map. They think that's a fake. . . . Right—the map that shows where pirate treasure is buried. . . .She's laughing again. What's so funny, Mrs. H.? . . . What? . . . She says she was pretty sure it was a fake, but she didn't want to spoil our fun. But how did you know? . . . She thinks it's a prop," reported Andy.

"What's a prop?" asked Hadia?

"It's like a dish or a book or something that an actor uses in a play, right Mom?" asked Sam.

"Yes, that's right. Andy, why does Millie think it's a prop?"

"Mom says why do you think it's a prop? . . . She says she thinks it was used in a play at the Rice Playhouse. Her parents used to make props for them. . . . Well no wonder we couldn't find any treasure! Where's the Rice Playhouse? . . . Oh, it burned down. Right after the—Wow!"

"Right after what, Andy?" demanded Hannah.

"After the murder! You're gonna have to tell us about that Mrs. H., but first, the diary is real. . . . Yeah, Mike Farnsworth says there's a man in Boston who wants to buy it for fifteen hundred dollars and then donate it to the museum. But we know it really belongs to you, so we're calling to ask if you want to sell it and if you do," Andy paused and swallowed hard, "where we should send the money?"

There was a long silence as Andy listened intently. "Yes, Mam. I understand. If that's what you want, that's what we'll . . . Yes, Mam, I understand. Can you send us a letter saying that you own the diary and that it's okay for us to do what you've asked? . . . Cool! . . . Gee, that would be swell. It sounds like a great story. . . . Okay and everybody here sends you theirs, too. Bye!"

A chorus of voices shouted questions as Andy hung up the phone.

"Hold on, hold on. Here's what she said. She said we should sell the diary and keep the money. She said she would just give it to a charity anyway."

"So we get to keep the money?" asked Sam in surprise.

"That's a lot of money," said Dan. "What do you think you'll do with it?"

"I think that will take some careful thought and perhaps a family council." suggested Rachel. "But right now, I think you guys should get to bed and I will run Hadia home."

"Oh, can't she spend the night, Mom? Please?"

"Would you like to stay, Hadia?"

"Oh, yes, Mrs. Bennett, if it would be all right—but I shall have to call Mrs. Dressler to ask if I may. Might I use your telephone?"

"Of course—you know where it is," said Rachel. As Hadia left the porch to phone, she added, "She has the loveliest manners."

"Hey, what about us? Our manners aren't too bad!" objected Sam.

"No, your manners are just fine," laughed Rachel. "You've obviously been very well brought up!"

Hadia returned from her phone call and said, "Mrs. Bennett I am sorry, but I must go home. My mother is going to call in an hour's time and I want so much to talk to her. Mrs. Dressler said she can come and get me if it is not convenient for you to take me home."

"It's no inconvenience at all, Hadia. Why don't you get your things and we'll be off."

"I'll get them for you," said Andy quickly, and he darted through the door.

"Goodness, who was that polite young man?" exclaimed Rachel and everyone laughed.

"What's so funny?" inquired Andy, as he returned with Hadia's things.

"Nothing, bro. Nothing at all," smiled Sam.

After farewells were made and plans discussed for the next meeting of *The Jolly Roger Club*, Rachel and Hadia headed off in the car. Dan took Hannah to the guest house leaving Sam and Andy alone together on the porch swing looking out at the sea.

"It sure is beautiful," observed Sam as the two rocked companionably in the swing. "I feel so close to Dad here, don't you?"

"I was just thinking that," Andy responded. "I can't believe it's been almost a year since—"

"I know. So much has happened. How do you think Mom is doing?"

"I think she's okay. She really likes her job, and I think she's happy with the way the house turned out."

"Yeah, but I think she must be awfully lonely. She and Dad used to spend so much time together—just talking about stuff. She doesn't have anyone to talk to now," said Sam.

"She can talk to us."

"Yeah, but it's not the same. I heard her on the phone with Gommy the other day. She said she was *content*, but that she wasn't sure she'd ever be really *happy* again. That made me so sad."

"It is sad," agreed Andy, "but on the other hand, it shows how happy she was with Dad and how much she loved him. I guess she wouldn't trade that for anything."

"My brother, the romantic! When did you grow up?"

"I guess we've both grown up a lot this past year," said Andy seriously. "We've had to. I hate that."

"I know—me, too. But think about what Hadia's been through. She lost her father, too, but she also had to leave her mom. Remember how hard it was for us those few weeks we were in New Jersey without Mom? And we knew she was okay and that we could talk to her whenever we wanted. Hadia can't even call home when she wants. Her mother has to go to the village store to use the phone."

"You're right. I'll stop complaining."

"Yeah right—that'll be the day," laughed Sam, ruffling her brother's hair.

"Cut it out! Come on, let's go to bed. I told Tom Potter I'd go wind surfing with him tomorrow."

"Andy—"

"Yeah?"

"I hope you won't mind my saying this, but I love you. I don't know how I would have gotten through this year without you. I'm so glad you're my twin."

Andy was silent for a time, looking out at the cobalt sky and the darkening sea. "Me too you," he said hoarsely. "You coming in?"

"I think I'll wait for Mom."

"Okay. 'Night," he said heading for the door after giving his beloved sister a kiss on the cheek. "You're the best, Sam."

Sam sat quietly, watching stars appear in the night sky.

"I miss you, Daddy. I think about you all the time. I hope you're somewhere nice. Somewhere you can watch over us and know how much we miss you and love you. If you are, please be extra careful to watch out for Mom. She misses you so much."

As Sam gathered up the empty pizza boxes and soda cans, Rachel's car pulled into the parking area on the side of the house.

"Hey kiddo," said Rachel as she climbed the steps to the porch. "Pretty night, huh?"

"Yeah," agreed Sam, "beautiful."

"But it's late, sweetie. Time for bed."

"I know. Mom—" she hesitated, "do you think it's crazy that I sometimes talk out loud to Daddy?"

"Well, if it is, you'd better call the looney bin. I talk to your Dad everyday."

"Good. I was afraid you didn't have anyone to talk to."

Rachel gave Sam a hug, gathered up the paper plates and napkins, and the two carried everything into the house. A moment later, the porch lights went out. Soon *Windswept* was completely dark, disappearing into the black velvet of the Vineyard night as a summer moon cut its silver path across the water.

36

As the summer drew to a close, the four friends began to prepare for the beginning of the school year. Expeditions for just the right notebooks and pencils were exercises in budgeting and careful shopping. At Dan's request, Sam took Hannah shopping for some new school clothes, and even Andy paid some attention to his wardrobe.

Rachel was busy finishing a house for a difficult client and came home late many nights as her Labor Day deadline for completing the job drew near. Dan filled in, putting simple meals together that all of them shared in the big dining room, now painted a lovely soft yellow. A fabric patterned with gold-finches covered the chairs and adorned the windows that overlooked the sound and the parkland which bordered the house.

Although Rachel and the kids joined in all the Labor Day weekend festivities, the approaching anniversary of the attacks on the World Trade Center was never far from their minds. Larry Binzen called Rachel after the holiday to say that a special September 11th assembly had been planned for school, and if she would like to keep Sam and Andy home, there would be no problem.

"I don't want to stay home!" cried Andy.

"Me neither. It's not like we don't know about it or like it won't be all over the news," agreed Sam.

"It's up to you entirely," Rachel assured them. "I think Mr. Binzen just wanted you to feel comfortable with whatever choice you made."

Just then, the phone rang and Sam was nearest, so she answered.

"Bennett residence, Sam speaking," she answered as she had been taught to do. "Oh, hi!" She covered the mouth piece.

"It's Mike Farnsworth," she told Andy and Rachel, then returned to the call. "Yes, this is Sam. . . . Really? That's great! . . . Yes, I think we can do that. Hang on, let me just ask Mom."

She held the phone against her chest and said, "He has the check for the diary. He wants to know if we can come and get it tomorrow afternoon. A reporter from the Gazette wants to take a picture of us getting it. Can we, Mom?"

"I don't see why not. Ask him what time," answered Rachel

"Mr. Farnsworth? Mom says we can come and wants to know what time. One o'clock?" Sam looked questioningly at Rachel who nodded her head. "Yes, that would be fine. . . . Oh, really? Well I'm not sure, but I'll talk to Andy. . . . Yes, sir. We'll see you then. And thank you very much. Bye." Sam hung up.

"What are you going to talk to me about?" asked Andy.

"He wants us to tell the reporter how we're going to use the money," replied Sam.

"Hmmm," mused Andy, "I'm not sure we're ready to do that."

"I didn't know you had decided," said Rachel, surprised that the twins hadn't shared their plans with her.

"It's kind of a secret for now, Mom," answered Sam mysteriously.

37

On the morning of September 11th, Rachel, Andy and Sam gathered very early and had a quiet breakfast together. They agreed that they did not want the television on. They did not want to hear the list of all the victims read aloud or hear the bell toll for their loss. Instead, they ate Ben's favorite breakfast—pecan waffles with maple syrup and sausage links. Then they sat together on the big sofa in the living room across from the portrait the twins had had painted for Rachel and looked through the photo albums she had made for them. When it was time to leave for school, the twins gathered their backpacks and joined Hannah in the car with Rachel. Although she was dreading it, Rachel had agreed to the twins request that she attend the special assembly.

Sam and Andy left Rachel in the lobby of the Oak Bluffs School and headed off to their classrooms. Their rooms were across the hall from each other and they gave each other a quick hug as they parted.

"See you in the auditorium," said Sam, fighting an overwhelming desire to burst into tears.

"Yup. Chin up, kiddo. It's only one day," whispered Andy.

Thankfully, both their teachers were well aware of their circumstances and avoided any discussion of the anniversary. The half hour before the assembly was spent turning in assignments and correcting math homework. A public address announcement informed them that it was time for the assembly and all the classes moved through the halls to the auditorium.

The program began with the Pledge of Allegiance and the singing of the national anthem. Principal Binzen read a letter from the Governor commemorating the anniversary. A group of eighth graders read essays they had written and there were several songs sung by different classes. Then Principal Binzen returned to the microphone.

"I am sure that most of you are aware that two of our students, Andy and Sam Bennett, lost their father on nine-eleven. They have asked permission to speak to you this morning, so please welcome to the stage, Andy and Sam Bennett."

Andy and Sam moved to the aisle and headed toward the stage. They were joined by Hannah and Hadia. As they moved forward, Sam glanced at Rachel seated with the other parents and smiled at the quizzical look on Rachel's face. When they reached the microphone, Sam took center stage.

"Thanks Mr. Binzen. This is a really hard day for Andy and me and our mom. But we wanted to honor our father and all the other men and women who lost their lives on nine-eleven."

Andy continued, "When we moved into our house here, we discovered an old diary and a map. We were hoping the map would lead us to buried pirate treasure," Andy paused as the audience laughed, "but there was no pirate treasure."

"We did find treasure though," Sam said as she took over. "We found something worth more than gold doubloons or jewels. We found friendship.

We've made all kinds of great new friends here, especially Hannah and Hadia. Their friendship has taught us two really important things. The first is that no matter how bad you think your life may be, there is always someone who is worse off. The other is that the most dangerous things in the world are not guns and bombs, but hate and fear."

Andy carried on. "That's what I felt when I first met Hadia. I was angry about what had happened to my dad and I needed someone to blame, so I blamed every Arab and every Muslim. Hadia taught me that we hate and fear the things we don't understand," admitted Andy. "We thought the best way to honor our dad and all the other people who died on nine-eleven was to find a way to help fight that hate."

"Thanks to Mike Farnsworth at the Museum," said Sam, "we learned that the diary we found was real and was worth a lot of money. For a while we thought about all the stuff we could buy, but then we realized that there was something better we could do with the money. One of the things we learned from Hadia is that in Afghanistan, it's really hard for girls to get a good education. That's why she was sent here—away from her family. We found out that there is a group that's building schools for girls in Afghanistan and other places, so we decided to give the money from the diary to this group," Sam paused for loud applause and then she continued, "but the little we can send isn't nearly enough, so we are hoping all of you will help us raise money to build schools for girls in Afghanistan and other places where girls can't go to school."

Andy went on. "We've got some ideas of how we could do it, but we'd like your suggestions, too. Sam and I think that helping educate the world's children about respect for other ideas would be the best way to make sure that another nine-eleven never happens. Thank you."

The auditorium erupted in applause and Sam and Andy looked toward Rachel, who, like the others, was on her feet applauding and smiling broadly.

Epilogue

Chappaquiddick, Martha's Vineyard, Massachusetts
October 1796

Gilbert Finlay felt a burning sensation in his left side. He had no idea where he was, but when he opened his eyes, it was almost totally dark and he could just make out the stripes on the sleeve of his shirt.

Confused, he struggled to figure our where he was and what was causing the pain in his side. A loud crash of thunder brought it all back to him. He knew the pain in his side was from the Captain's pistol! He realized he was lying on his stomach with his face resting on his arm. He could feel sand under his hand. But why couldn't he lift his head? Panic gripped him as he realized that he was buried. Buried alive!

With all the strength he had, Gilbert Finlay turned on his side and began scratching his way to the surface of his grave. Thankfully, it was a fairly shallow grave and within minutes he felt his hand break through the surface. Just as he was about to push up through the sand, he stopped.

He had no idea how long he had lain there. What if the Captain was still there on the shore? No sense getting shot twice in one night. Gilbert carefully and slowly pushed away the sand a little at a time until he could raise his head through the hole. As his eyes adjusted to the storm ravaged sky, Gilbert took a great long gulp of the sea air. Nothing had ever smelled so good to him.

He carefully scanned the beach, and after a moment, he could see that the great ship had hoisted anchor and was far off the coast heading to open water. Gilbert pushed more sand away until he could move his upper body, and he dragged himself from the grave. He caught his breath as a stab of pain coursed through him. He felt his left side with his hand and came away with bloody fingers. Gritting his teeth he probed the area until he was sure that the

Captain's bullet had only grazed his side. Thankfully, the Captain had never been a very good shot.

It was only then that he heard a soft moaning and turned to see the body of his companion, Henry Smithwick, shift slightly. Gilbert crouched by Henry. Even in the dim light of the beach, he could tell that Henry was in a bad way. Then he saw the bloom of red from the center of Henry's shirt.

"Henry, lad, can you hear me?" asked Gilbert.

"Aye. It's bad, isn't it?" Henry whispered.

"Well, it ain't good, mate, but try to hang on. I'll see if I can find some help."

"I'll do me best, laddie. But don't take too long."

With that, Gilbert headed down the beach hoping to find a house where someone might be able to offer some help. After many minutes of difficult hiking, Gilbert saw a small cabin on a rise above the beach. The house was dark and despite loud banging, no one responded. Discouraged, he headed back down to the shore to continue his search. It was then that he saw the small boat, secured to the beach by a large rock. Without a thought that he was stealing someone's property (he was, after all, a pirate), Gilbert launched the small craft and began rowing back to where Henry Smithwick lay wounded.

Twenty minutes later he beached the boat and headed toward the dunes. His sense of direction was excellent, and within a few minutes he stood beside the open grave.

"Henry—Henry, I'm back," announced Gilbert. But Henry did not respond. Gilbert knelt by his friend and felt his neck for a pulse. There was none and Henry's lifeless eyes stared up at him unseeing.

"Oh, Henry, mate—'tis a big sea you're sailing now! Fair wind, old friend."

Gilbert gently pulled Henry's body from the grave and placed it carefully in the little boat. He rowed out to deep water and sent Henry over the side where he would have wanted to be.

As he sat drifting in the boat, Gilbert wondered what he should do now. He had no ship, no family, and no home. Well, he did have one thing. He had the Captain's treasure chest. Its contents would be enough to set him up in a small business somewhere and keep him comfortable for the rest of his life. With that thought, he began to row back to the shore.

Acknowledgements

irst and foremost, I must thank Jim Smith and Carl Condit of Sunstone Press for taking a chance on a sixty-something, first time author and for all their efforts in preparing the manuscript for publication. Thanks also to my dear friend, Rick Herrick, who introduced me to them and who read my manuscript and gave me insightful advice. I also thank Nancy Slonim Aronie of the Chilmark Writing Workshop who taught me to write from my heart. I am grateful to Margie Davis, retired Children's Librarian from East Greenwich, Rhode Island, who read and critiqued the manuscript; Hillary Wall, librarian for the Vineyard Gazette for help with research; Steve Zablotny who provided technical assistance; Sam and Lucia Beer for teaching me how a calf is born; and many friends and colleagues who have offered encouragement and moral support! Last but not least, my husband Fred: my best friend and my most ardent supporter, who always believes in me even when I don't believe in myself.

Readers Guide

1. The title of this book is *Windswept*. What do you think of when you hear that something is *windswept*? Besides the name of the house, how does the title relate to the story?

2. Andy and Sam are twins and have a great deal in common, but they are also very different. Compare and contrast Andy and Sam.

3. Discuss the roles Rachel, Sam and Andy each play in helping the family to recover from the loss of Ben?

4. A *legacy* is a gift which one receives from someone who has died. It may be money or a physical object like the house, but it can also be an idea or belief. Besides the house, what was Ben's legacy for his family? How did it help them to heal? Be sure to consider Gommy and Gompy as well as Rachel and the twins.

5. Putting aside gender, who would you choose as a friend, Andy or Sam? Why? Give specific examples to support your opinion.

6. The twins convince Rachel to let them move to the Vineyard sooner than she had planned. How might the story have changed if she hadn't made that decision?

7. What factors influence Andy to change his mind about Hadia?

8. Why do Sam, Andy, Hannah and Hadia make such a good team? What does each contribute to the team's success?

9. Was it right of Gilbert to keep the treasure? Why or why not?

10. If there was a sequel to this book, what do you think would happen?

CPSIA information can be obtained at www.ICGtesting.com
Printed in the USA
BVOW02s1320090715

407333BV00001B/11/P